sleuth or dare

Partners in Crime

sleuth or dare

sleuth or dare

Partners in Crime

Kim Harrington

Scholastic Inc.

NEW YORK   TORONTO   LONDON   AUCKLAND

SYDNEY   MEXICO CITY   NEW DELHI   HONG KONG

ISBN 978-0-545-38964-8

12 11 10 9 8 7 6 5   13 14 15 16 17/0

Printed in the U.S.A.   40

First edition, May 2012

Book design by Tim Hall

sleuth or dare

Partners in Crime

Chapter

The killer held his breath and huddled in the back of the darkened closet, hoping not to be found. But the woman with the wire-rimmed glasses paused and tilted her head to the side. A floorboard squeak, followed by the rattle of a hanger, told her that something — or *someone* — was in the closet. She stepped forward, one hand reaching out for the doorknob, and —

"Will you shut that thing off?" I said, looking over Darcy's shoulder.

"Norah! It's just getting to the good part!" Darcy protested.

I reached over and closed her laptop. "You shouldn't be watching those horror shows anyway. You'll have nightmares."

Darcy ran her hand through the purple streak in her short black hair, which matched her outfit. Her entire wardrobe was black and purple.

"First off," she began, "it's not horror. It's my favorite detective show, *Crime Scene: New York*. Second, I never get nightmares. Third, it's ten thousand times better than those sleep-inducing astronomy documentaries you watch. And fourth, I like to try to figure out the ending. Why won't you let me have any fun?"

"Because we have work to do." I sighed. "Can we get back to it, please?"

Darcy gave me the stink eye. With love, of course, because we're best friends.

I sat back down, slid an elastic off my wrist, and pulled my long blond hair up into a ponytail. Darcy and I were in my room, sitting opposite each other on my polka-dotted beanbag chairs. My room is my favorite place in the world. I have cool astronomy posters on the walls and glow-in-the-dark stars on my ceiling, which are an exact replica of the night sky in October when Orion — my favorite constellation — is most visible.

Darcy and I were supposed to be working on our social studies project: creating a small business. Not a real one — we're seventh graders. But we were supposed to come up with the name, logo, and a little business plan. And then we had to present it in front of our teacher, Mrs. Feldman, and the whole class (gulp!) in one week. But we couldn't even get started on the assignment until we decided what that business should be. It was stressing me out just a little.

I looked at the ideas I'd written in my notebook.

"How about a dog walking company? Or pet sitting?" I suggested.

"Meh," Darcy said and blew a giant purple bubble with her gum.

I leaned forward and popped it with my finger. The remnants of the bubble stuck to her chin. "Why don't *you* come up with a good idea, then?" I asked her.

"I have." Darcy crossed her arms.

I rolled my eyes. "We need something *legal*."

Darcy and I are both nerds and proud of it, but I use my brainpower for good. Darcy, on the other hand . . . Hmm, how should I say this? You know how compasses always lead north? Darcy's moral compass leads to trouble. Everyone says I'm a "good influence" on her. I try to keep her from going too far over to the

Dark Side, but some days I'm convinced she's one computer hack from being led away in handcuffs.

Darcy Carter moved into the house next door three years ago, when we were in fourth grade. My mom, model neighbor that she is, baked brownies and insisted we walk over as a family to welcome the new people to the neighborhood. Darcy and her mom answered the door. Darcy gratefully grabbed the plate of treats while her mother blushed and gave an embarrassed smile.

You see, Darcy's beautiful black hair looked like it'd been cut by a lawn mower. It stuck out at all angles around her face. I'd assumed she was a deranged moron.

I still believe the deranged part. But, as I quickly learned in school, Darcy is smart. Really smart. Like maybe, possibly, just a tiny bit smarter than me. (And she told me later that she'd hacked all her hair off like that on purpose to protest her mother's decision to move out of Boston and to our "boring little town" of Danville, Massachusetts.)

One day, several weeks after they moved in, Darcy came over and knocked on my door. Her hair had grown to a short bob, but one section was streaked purple. Apparently she was only half protesting then.

She said, "Well, it looks like I'm stuck in this town, and you're the only kid in school I could ever imagine myself hanging with, so . . . want to be friends?"

I didn't know what to say to that. I think I stood there and blinked a few times. Then Darcy held out her fist . . . for the first of a million times in our friendship.

"Give it a jab," she said.

"Um, okay." I made a fist and bumped hers.

"Cool," she said. Then she walked into my house and we raided the kitchen for cookies.

We've been best friends ever since.

Now we sat rubbing our foreheads, struggling to think of a great idea.

"We need to be different," Darcy said. "Everyone is going to do something typical like a babysitting company or a lemonade stand."

That was true. And, honestly, the idea of gluing pictures onto yet another poster board was so boring, it made me want to puke. Darcy and I like a challenge.

I glanced over at Darcy's shut laptop. She always brings her computer when she comes to my house. She needs to be connected at all times. Most people breathe air. Darcy breathes Internet.

I have a computer, but my parents don't allow me to keep it in my room. It's in the living room, where they can watch me and make sure I don't get into any trouble. Me. Miss Has Never Been In Trouble.

(Meanwhile, Darcy, who gets in trouble on a regular basis, could ask her mother if she could keep a nuclear reactor in her room and her mother would say yes.)

But the sight of Darcy's beloved laptop gave me a flash of inspiration. "How about we do a website for the business?" I suggested, sitting up straight. "I can design the logo and do the writing for the site. You can do the programming!"

Darcy rose up from the beanbag chair, her eyes wide with excitement. "And on presentation day, you can talk to the class, and I can handle the tech stuff to make the website come up on the big screen." She sat back down and immediately opened her laptop.

I nodded, grinning. "That will be so cool." Then I frowned. "But we're still no closer to picking a business." I threw my arms down to my sides. "We need help."

"Help . . ." Darcy repeated in a whisper. She looked at her laptop screen, which showed a paused image from the crime show she'd been watching. Then her whole face lit up and she turned to me. "I got it! A detective agency. Our fake business will be a detective agency!"

"Detectives?" I said, feeling hesitant. "Us?"

"Think about it," Darcy said. "It's a business that's mysterious and edgy, so that's perfect for me. But it exists to help people, which appeals to you, the big goody-goody."

"Gee, thanks," I said, but I was smiling. I did like the idea of a business that helped people. But I wasn't obsessed with crime shows like Darcy was. I didn't even read mystery books. What did I know about running a detective agency?

"But what would I even put on the website? Or say in the presentation?" I asked.

"Oh, that's easy! Watch one episode of *Crime Scene: New York* with me, and you'll learn so much!"

I bit my lip. I'd never seen Darcy so enthusiastic about a project before. And we didn't have any better ideas. And it was due in a week. . . .

My mom called up from downstairs. "Norah! Time to eat! Darcy, are you staying for dinner?"

"No, thank you, Mrs. Burridge!" Darcy yelled out the open doorway. "So what do you think?" she asked me.

7

I nodded quickly before I could change my mind. "Sure. A detective agency. Let's do it."

Mom made spaghetti and meatballs for dinner — my favorite — and I totally pigged out. She always complained that I "ate like a bird," never realizing that if she'd just make spaghetti and meatballs, say . . . three nights a week, it would make up for all the other nights I picked at her vegetables and over-cooked chicken.

Most nights I slipped half my dinner under the table to Hubble. That's my dog. I named him after the world's most famous telescope. My parents wanted to name him Fluffybean. Seriously. Fluffybean. It was one of those moments when I questioned who the grown-ups are here and who's the kid.

For years, my parents told me we could never have a dog because I have allergies. But, last year, I did some research on my own, called a family meeting, and presented my case. I'd found that there are certain breeds that are almost hypoallergenic. Also, they don't shed. (I said this in a very dramatic voice while looking straight at my mother. I knew that fact would

8

appeal to the clean freak in her.) My pitch was so good, my parents couldn't say no. And now we have Hubble. He's a goofy little guy with brown fur. You know Chewbacca from *Star Wars*? Picture him fifteen pounds and a dog and that's Hubble.

He sat under the table and stared at me with his tongue hanging out. I shook my head. He wasn't getting any secret food slipped to him tonight. This spaghetti was all mine. I slurped it up happily while my parents talked about their day and made googly eyes at each other.

My mom and dad were prom king and queen in their high school. For reals. She was the perky blond cheerleader (that's where I get my hair). And he was the star football player (that's where I get my height). But other than shared physical characteristics, we have nothing in common. Dad is a mailman and lives for sports. Mom teaches at a dance studio and loves fashion and makeup. Meanwhile, I spend my days on advanced mathematics and my nights staring through my telescope. I don't know how I came into being. Sometimes I don't think my parents know, either, because every now and then when I mention some astronomical fact, they look at me like I'm an alien.

"How did that math test go this week, honey?" Dad asked as we cleared the table.

"I got an A," I said, handing him my dish and fork.

He patted the top of my head. "As always, kiddo."

But I wasn't sure I'd do as well on my social studies project. Was a detective agency *too* different? Plus, the thought of presenting in front of everyone was enough to make me want to start biting my nails.

I took Hubble for a quick walk, then headed back into the kitchen, thinking I'd get some ice cream. My parents were supposed to be doing dishes, but instead I walked in on a lip lock.

"Eww, guys!" I screeched. "That's gross."

They rolled their eyes in unison. Mom said, "Norah, we're married. We're in love. We kiss. Get over it."

"Well, I just vomited in my mouth and swallowed it," I said, retreating from the kitchen. I didn't want dessert anymore.

Listen, I realize people kiss. And that's cool. But parents should not kiss. Especially not in a kitchen, where some unsuspecting child could walk in. Please. Think of the children.

The phone rang. The house phone, because my parents won't let me have a cell. Meanwhile, Darcy has the latest iPhone, a landline in her room, *and* an untraceable TracFone she bought off eBay (for what, I don't even *want* to know).

I answered, and right away Darcy said, "Have you thought of any names for our detective agency?"

"Oh," I said, feeling guilty. I should have been thinking of one, but instead I'd been getting nervous thinking about the presentation. "How about, um, The Girls Detective Agency?" I offered.

"Ehhhh," Darcy said. "I want something that says we work together on your case . . . but also something with a little oomph."

I sighed. *Something that says we work together . . .* "Okay, how about The Partners Agency?"

Darcy took in a sharp breath. "That's it!"

"Huh?" I didn't think it was so great, honestly. I was just tossing ideas out there.

"Partners in Crime!" Darcy yelled.

I grinned. As nervous as I was about this whole detective agency thing, I had to admit . . . that name? I kind of liked it.

Chapter

2

One week later, we were in Mrs. Feldman's class a few minutes before the bell, setting up for our big presentation. I stood stiffly in front of all the empty desks, trying to look confident. But the note cards in my hands were trembling. My stomach felt like I'd just stumbled off one of those looping roller coasters.

It didn't help that Darcy was on her hands and knees, snarling and mumbling something about a cheap cable. She grabbed her backpack and pulled another wire out. My eyes went to the wall clock. Two minutes. If we couldn't get the website to come up, we had nothing to show for our presentation. We might fail!

Just as I was wondering if we should have gone the

simple route like everyone else, Darcy waved her fist in the air and said, "Yes!"

"Are we all set?" I whispered. A few kids had already rolled in and were seated and waiting.

"Yep. We're all connected. After you introduce the company, I'll flip the projector on."

Fiona Fanning, fashionista of the seventh grade, strolled into the room. She wore a stylish pink dress and gray wedges, and carried her little pink notebook under one arm. Fiona may look like she just walked off the cover of a teen magazine, but she has the brains of a doorknob. She raised her eyebrows at the sight of Darcy with her laptop. "I guess it's Taco Day," she sneered, and the other kids chuckled.

This little joke stemmed from the time Darcy hacked into the school's system and changed the monthly lunch menu so that every day was Taco Day. For thirty days.

Darcy likes tacos.

Mrs. Feldman clapped her hands loudly to get the attention of the class. "I'm sure you've all worked very hard on your team projects, and I'm excited to see what you've come up with. Norah and Darcy have asked to go first since their presentation requires equipment. So take it away, Norah and Darcy!"

She attempted to lead the class in an enthusiastic round of clapping, but half of them were already falling asleep.

I cleared my throat and began to speak. "For our assignment . . ." My voice was too quiet. I tried again, louder and stronger. "For our assignment, we decided to create a website to advertise our small business."

I glanced at Darcy, who nodded and flipped the switch on the projector. The website lit up the big screen on the wall. "Presenting . . . Partners in Crime. A detective agency!" she said.

The class sat up a bit straighter and actually — gasp — started paying attention. This gave me a little jolt of confidence. I smiled and straightened my shoulders. "As you can see, we created a website and a logo for our business. We have a page about what the company does. And a contact page so people can ask the detective agency for help."

The home page was black and white with our logo in the center. Darcy had wanted two girls holding handcuffs. I thought that was a bit over the top, so I'd suggested a magnifying glass. She gave me directions to the nearest old folks' home in response. So we compromised with an image of a fingerprint and the words *Partners in Crime* underneath. I thought it looked pretty cool up there.

The ABOUT US page featured a list of the types of cases the agency would take on. Things like surveillance, missing persons, theft investigations, and background checks. (We'd watched a few episodes of Darcy's favorite crime show and took notes to get the words right.) CONTACT US led to a form Darcy had built in with white boxes for name, e-mail, and reason for contacting.

All in all, I thought we did a great job. I talked about how the agency would help people, and before I knew it, my required three minutes were up. I didn't even need to glance down at my note cards because I'd practiced it ten thousand times with Darcy.

Mrs. Feldman applauded when we finished. "Wonderful work, Norah and Darcy! I actually wish your small business *was* real."

Back at our desks, Darcy held out her fist and I bumped it. Then I breathed a sigh of relief. This whole project was done.

My racing heart slowed back to normal as the rest of the teams presented their work. Maya Doshi and Slade Durkin had come up with a pet-sitting business. Maya was the smallest and quietest girl in class. She had just moved to town this year when her parents opened up a popular Indian restaurant. She stood behind the desk and shyly held up the poster board advertising the business. The only part of her showing was the bump of her high ponytail. Her partner, Slade, was the loudest kid. He often burped the alphabet and farted with his armpit at inappropriate times. Normally, I'd feel bad for Maya, since she got partnered with him. (Assigning partners alphabetically had worked out for Darcy and me.) But it may have made the presentation easier on her since Slade was more than willing to do all the talking.

I kind of spaced during the next couple of presentations, until Zane Munro stood up. He walked to the front of the class all alone because his partner was sick. I straightened in my seat and gave him a smile to try to put him at ease. He returned it with a nervous grin and, even though he had a mouth full of braces, he was still so cute. Zane has sandy brown hair and wears T-shirts every day, even in winter when I wear long-sleeve thermals under my sweaters.

As he started talking about his business — a soccer program for little kids — it was obvious that he felt as nervous as I had up there. I didn't know what was shaking more, his voice or his hands. I thought there was a distinct possibility that his presentation would end with him puking on his shoes.

To make matters worse, Hunter Fisk kept making faces at him. Hunter did this disgusting thing where he flipped his eyelids inside out. And, of course, poor Zane couldn't concentrate and kept losing his place in his presentation.

I tapped Hunter's shoulder with my pencil. "That's rude," I said. "Stop it."

But Hunter enjoys being mean as much as Darcy enjoys tacos, so Zane's presentation ended with a spitball to his forehead. Carefully timed by Hunter to a moment when Mrs. Feldman's back was turned, of course.

Unbeknownst to the rest of us, though, Darcy had crept down to Hunter's feet like a stealth ninja, untied his right shoe, and retied the shoelace to the chair. So when the bell rang and Hunter stood up, he took his chair with him, tripped, and landed on his face.

Darcy held her fist out.

I gave it a bump.

AFTER school, we hung in my room as usual. Darcy flopped onto a beanbag and opened her laptop. I unzipped my backpack and pulled out my folder.

"What homework are you doing first?" I asked.

"I don't have any," Darcy said, tapping her fingers while waiting for her computer to start up.

"What about the book report?" I asked.

"Done."

"Math?"

"Calculated."

"Spanish?"

"Translated."

"You haven't even opened your backpack yet, Darcy. How is all your homework already done?"

She counted off on her fingers. "I did the book report during math class, my math in Spanish, and my Spanish in English."

I sighed and slid out my first assignment.

"I can just give you my math and you can copy it," Darcy said, smirking because she already knew what I was going to say. I'd never cheat. I was about to remind her of that fact, but she suddenly sat up straight, stared at her screen, and said, "Whoa."

"What?" I asked.

She looked up from the computer and met my eyes. "The website we created for our fake detective agency just got an e-mail about a real case."

Chapter

3

My heart started pounding. A *real* case? I thought the contact form was just boxes on the website page. I didn't think it actually worked.

"How is that possible?" I asked.

"When I created the form on the contact page, it needed to lead to a real e-mail address. So I just had it forwarded to mine." Darcy shrugged as if this was nothing.

"And someone actually used the form and sent us a message about a case?"

Darcy nodded, grinning. "Isn't it awesome?"

"That depends," I said, feeling slightly nervous. "What does the message say?"

Darcy spun the laptop around to face me. "See for yourself."

I squinted at the screen. The e-mail address looked fake. happypanda4444? Seriously, who would choose that? The space for the name was blank. My eyes shot down to the message, and goose bumps sprang up all over my arms. It was only one line:

Please find my twin sister.

I gasped. "What does that mean?"

"It means this person has a twin who's missing, and he or she wants us to find her," Darcy replied sarcastically.

"Obviously." I rolled my eyes. "But was she kidnapped? Did she run away? Were they separated somehow? 'Find my sister' could mean a whole bunch of things."

Darcy tapped her chin with a black-painted fingernail. "True, that." A slow smile spread across her face. "We'll have to write back."

I grabbed her hand before she could start typing. "What are you going to say?"

"That we need more information before we can agree to take the case." She pulled her hand away and raised it over the keyboard.

Take on the case?! "Wait, Darcy," I said.

The website was only supposed to be a school project. We'd do the work, get the grade, and move on to the next thing. I never intended to get involved in a real mystery!

Darcy, of course, felt no hesitation. Her eyes were practically glowing. "Come on, Norah," she said, flexing her fingers like they were itching to start typing.

"We're not real detectives," I argued. "We're — not, you know, qualified."

"Whoever wrote this *knows* that," Darcy explained. "No one outside of our social studies class — well, outside of our school — could have seen this website."

I raised my eyebrows in suspicion. "If it's on the Internet, anyone could have seen it."

"Well . . ." Darcy looked up at the ceiling. She always has trouble with eye contact when she's busted doing something bad. "I didn't want to pay for web hosting, so I sort of . . . hacked into the school's server and used their space. So it's only up on the school's intranet. Nowhere else."

"The what?" I said.

"In-TRA-net. It's like a private network that the school uses, and you can only access it there."

Although Darcy didn't ask permission before she stole school server space, I wasn't interested in lecturing her now. I wanted to figure out what was going on.

"Hmm," I said. "That does narrow down the list of who could've sent the message." But still . . . us? Solving a *real* case? That was crazy. "I don't know if we should get involved."

Darcy said, "This person needs help, and our presentation gave them the idea to turn to us. To put their trust in us. You *do* want to help a classmate in need, don't you?" Darcy smiled. She knew what buttons to press on me.

I did enjoy a challenge. And if someone really did need help . . .

I stared up at the plastic stars on my ceiling. Darcy and I were both only children. I thought about what it would be like to have a sibling — let alone a twin — and then have them . . . disappear. If that's what even happened. It must be maddening to have a sister and not know where she is. And to ask for the help of two seventh graders, the person must be . . . desperate. My heart went out to whoever he or she was.

"Okay," I said. "Write back. Ask for more info."

Darcy's fingers flew over the keyboard as she typed.

Who are you?

What happened to your sister?

We might help. . . .

She paused for a moment, then hit SEND.

"Now what?" I asked.

"Now," Darcy said, lacing her hands behind her head, "we wait."

After a couple minutes of sitting in stunned silence, I decided to get back to my homework. There was a chance the mystery e-mailer wouldn't write back at all. I couldn't sit around forever waiting for a —

Ding!

My eyes widened. "Is that what I think it is?"

A devilish look came over Darcy's face. "I have new mail."

I scrambled off the beanbag and over to Darcy's side as quickly as I could. She clicked on the message.

It listed a name, a birth date, and the line *Find her.*

"Bailey Ann Banks, Bailey Ann Banks." I repeated

the name a few times. It meant nothing to me. I eyeballed Darcy.

She shrugged. "Never heard of her." She frowned at the screen. "And this doesn't really answer the two questions I asked."

"Maybe that's the only information the person has," I said.

A thousand questions darted through my head. Who was Bailey? Why was she missing? Had she lived here in town? Why was our e-mailer staying anonymous? Why did he or she contact us instead of the police? I didn't even know where to begin.

"But whose twin could she be?" Darcy said, looking frustrated. "There's no one with the last name Banks in our social studies class. Or even our *grade*."

I squinted at the screen. "Maybe the name was changed or something," I mused out loud. "Or maybe it's someone in a different grade."

"But check out her birthday," Darcy said.

"April fourth. So?"

Darcy pointed. "The *year*."

I blinked quickly as I realized it. "She's our age." A shiver went down my back.

"Yeah." Darcy nodded. "Since this person is looking for their twin, it means this person *has* to be in our grade."

"What do we do now?" I asked, scratching my head.

Darcy picked at the paint on her thumbnail. "I think the first thing we need to figure out is who our mystery e-mailer is."

I nodded, and flipped to a fresh page in my notebook. "Maybe we should make a list of suspects?" Darcy and I like making lists.

Darcy was staring at me, her eyes sparkling. "So you're saying we should take the case?"

I took a deep breath, wondering if we were ready for all this. "I think so."

Darcy nodded eagerly. "I agree, Detective."

Chapter 4

Darcy and I never got around to making our suspect list because my mom had called me down for dinner. The next day, I had trouble paying attention in school. Me. Miss Always Pays Attention. But the mystery of Bailey Ann Banks wouldn't leave my head.

At lunch, I put my tray down and started to dig into the spaghetti. I love Pasta Day. It's the only day I buy the hot lunch. Darcy settled in beside me and ripped open her paper lunch bag to reveal a juice box, a Ring Ding, a Twinkie, and a Ho Ho. I raised an eyebrow.

"What?" she said. "The boxes were expiring tomorrow. I'm doing my mom a favor. We wouldn't want to have to throw it out and waste food."

"Twinkies expire?" I said doubtfully.

Darcy ignored my question. "So," she whispered, "I started on that list."

I glanced around nervously. Talking about suspects right in the middle of the cafeteria gave me butterflies in my stomach. Not the good kind like when a cute boy (um, Zane) smiles at you. More the nasty butterflies-with-fangs kind.

"I don't know," I said. "Let me focus on getting through the school day. We *do* have an English quiz after lunch."

Darcy waved her hand as if that wasn't important. "But what about the investigation?"

I glanced over my shoulder. "It's too risky to talk about it here at school. We'll pick that back up this afternoon."

She took a huge bite of a Ring Ding and thought it over. After some chewing, she said, "Only if we can meet at my house this time."

I sighed. "Deal."

I did well on the English quiz, so I was much less stressed by the time we climbed the stairs to Darcy's room that afternoon. Our homes were almost identical from the outside. But inside, they couldn't be more different. Darcy's bedroom walls were all dark purple except for the one behind her bed, which was black. Darcy and her mother liked modern-looking furniture, but to me, most of it just looked weird.

I slid onto a wavy-styled chair that looked like a strip of bacon. "So let's see the list."

Darcy took out her notebook and opened it to a page of names. "I wrote down everyone who was in class the day of our presentation. It could be a boy or a girl because the e-mailer didn't say they were identical twins." She shrugged. "Let's figure it out!"

I attempted to lean forward, but the bacon chair wouldn't let me. "Who's first on the list?"

Darcy shoved me over a bit so we could share the bacon chair. Thankfully, it was big enough for two. "Maya Doshi," Darcy said, pointing at the name. "She was very quiet that day."

"Maya's always quiet," I said. "I think I've only heard her speak two words in my entire life." I looked at the list. "What about Fiona Fanning?"

"Please." Darcy rolled her eyes. "That girl has more shoes than brain cells. She wouldn't think to e-mail us from the website."

Darcy's finger trailed along the list of names and stopped at one. "What about Zane Munro? Did you see how nervous he was during the presentations?"

Zane? No way, I thought. "He was nervous because he had to stand in front of the class by himself, and Hunter Fisk kept shooting spitballs at his head. Plus, he wouldn't bother with all the secrecy. If he wanted my help, he'd just ask."

Darcy tilted her head to the side and said in a singsong voice, "Norah likes Za-ane . . ."

"Darcy, stop it."

"You want Zane to be your boyyy frieeend."

I crossed my arms. "Shut up. Next suspect."

Darcy let out one last laugh, then moved on. "Speaking of Hunter, he was firing death rays at me from his eyeballs today."

"You tied his shoelace to the chair and made him fall in front of the entire class."

"Oh yeah," Darcy said, smiling. "I guess his evil stare could've been because of that."

"Slade was sweating a lot today in social studies," I said. "Sweating could be a sign of guilty secret keeping."

"Or it could be that Slade always sweats." Darcy made a face. "He's wetter than a dog's nose."

We went through the rest of the class list, but it all ended the same. No real clues, just guesses. Darcy started to pull at her hair and it stuck out at odd angles. "Well, that was a waste of time," she said. "We're never going to figure out who our client is."

But while Darcy was trying to look for clues in our classmates' behavior, an idea occurred to me.

"Wait." I shot up from the bacon chair excitedly. "It's all about the numbers!"

Darcy tilted her head like Hubble does when he's confused.

"The birth date!" I said.

Darcy's eyes lit up as she caught on. "You're right! The twin was born on April fourth. So all we need to do is find out which one of our classmates was born on April fourth."

But the excitement drained from my body as I said out loud, "Err, how do we do that?"

Darcy thought for a moment, then a smile stole across her face. "I have an idea."

Oh no. I could see trouble brewing. "What's your plan?" I asked.

"We go to Principal Plati's office and wait until he isn't around. Then we do something to distract the secretary. She leaves the office unattended. Then I slip inside, download the seventh-grade student file onto a flash drive, and we'll have a listing of everyone's birthdays."

"Darcy!" I cried. "You can't mess around in the school office again. You'll be suspended."

Last year, once a month, Darcy snuck into the office and inserted "Happy Birthday to Darcy Carter" into Principal Plati's morning announcements. The school secretary figured out after four months that something was up, but I think Principal Plati would have gone on wishing Darcy a happy birthday for a few more months after that.

"It's the fastest way," Darcy argued.

"You *can't* do it," I said, worry leaking into my voice. We joked around about us being opposites and it *was* fun that Darcy wasn't always a goody-goody like me. But this was going over the line. I pleaded with my eyes. Darcy was my best friend and I didn't want her constantly getting into trouble.

Darcy heaved a sigh. "Fine. We'll find another way."

I leaned back in the chair and let out the breath I'd been holding. "Thank you."

Chapter

5

We couldn't research our classmates' birthdays over the weekend. But I had a different kind of birthday to deal with: my cousin's third birthday party, which was about as awful as you could imagine. My aunt and uncle hired a clown and, long story short, twenty little kids are now traumatized for life.

One of the kids was apparently terrified of clowns. He started screaming as soon as the clown entered the room with his big floppy shoes and red bulbous nose. The clown made the mistake of reaching for the scared boy, maybe to try to make him feel better. But all the kids immediately got it into their preschool brains that the clown was about to kill them. So they all started screaming and running around the house.

This then ruined our weekly family movie night because my mom had a migraine.

So, instead, I headed upstairs to read for a while. It was a good book, from one of my favorite sci-fi authors. But I couldn't concentrate. My mind kept wandering to Bailey Ann Banks, whoever or wherever she was. I walked over to the window and trailed my fingers along my all-time favorite birthday present — my telescope. I leaned over and peered through the lens. The moon wasn't full yet, but I still had a nice view of the seas. (Those are the moon's dark spots. But they're not *actual* seas. They're plains of solidified lava.)

Most kids our age don't really know what they want to be when they grow up. They're just guessing. Darcy says she'll end up as either an FBI agent or a fugitive permanently on the run.

But I've always known what I want to be. An astronomer. I want to study the skies, the stars, and the planets. I want to solve the mysteries of the universe. When some people come up against a scientific unanswered question, they get frustrated. They want to know "why" right now. Me? I'm delighted. It's a challenge, set out there ready and waiting for me.

I wondered if maybe that was why I was starting to get excited about this missing twin sister case. At first, Darcy had been more into it than I was. But now it was all I could think about.

I wanted us to solve this mystery.

And we would.

ON Monday, Darcy and I kept to our vow not to discuss the case at school. But it was clearly killing us. At lunch, we silently shared a plate of French fries, feeling tense. Finally, Darcy spoke up, but it was only to ask if I wanted ketchup. I did, so she jumped up and headed to the condiments table.

I gazed around the cafeteria. Maya Doshi was, as always, sitting alone. Her pretty, long black hair covered her face as she leaned over a book. Maya had no friends that I knew of. I'd tried talking to her a couple times, but she always seemed so nervous, like my questions were tests. She's really shy.

I thought about how hard it must be. Talking is as easy to some people as math is to me. But others have to work at it. So Maya wasn't talkative; that wasn't her fault. But, because she was so quiet, it was like she was invisible. No one even looked at her most of the time.

Behind Maya, Zane was sitting one table over with his friends. I sighed inwardly.

Zane is not the most gorgeous boy in school. He's not the smartest or funniest. And though he's great at soccer, that's his only sport (as the other jocks remind him). But he *is* the kindest boy. I've never seen him bully or make fun of anyone. He treats everyone the same, whether you're popular or a giant dork. And that is really, really cool.

The problem, though, with a boy who's nice to everyone is that there's no way to tell if he likes you back. You know . . . *likes* you, likes you. Not that I like him. But if I did, it would be difficult to see if he liked me back. That's all I'm saying.

As if he could feel me staring, Zane turned and looked right at me. I shot my eyes downward, but there was nothing I could do about the red blush that I'm sure was lighting up my face and neck.

After a minute, I peeked over my shoulder to see what was taking Darcy so long. Surprisingly, she seemed to be chatting with Fiona Fanning.

Fiona was wearing a skirt and high-heeled booties. Her long brown hair has blond highlights she swears are natural, but she must spend an hour every morning with a flatiron to make every strand look just so. Meanwhile, my blond hair has more of the "wash, blow-dry, and go" look to it. I don't spend much time on my appearance. But that's probably why every boy in the seventh grade has a crush on Fiona, and I've never even had a boy call my house or slip me a note.

Fiona is totally stuck-up, with her popular friends and all that. I could only imagine what insulting thing she was saying to Darcy now. I hoped Darcy had some self-control. I'd just talked her out of one trip to the principal's office on Friday.

When Darcy returned to the table with packets of ketchup, I asked her, "What was the beauty queen bugging you about?"

"Nothing really," Darcy said, looking confused. "She was just complaining about how Mrs. Feldman's class was so boring today."

The fry fell from my fingers. "Wait, wait, wait. . . . Fiona Fanning was just . . . nice to you?"

"Yeah." Darcy reached around the air with her hands. "There's a disturbance in the force."

We laughed, but then the bell rang and I wasn't laughing anymore. Time for gym. I hated gym. Darcy and I were always picked last.

"Time to go," I said with a groan.

We started moving out of the cafeteria with the crowd. Hunter Fisk sneered at us as we walked by, and Darcy stuck her tongue out at him.

Suddenly, Darcy grabbed my elbow and whispered, "I know we said we wouldn't talk about *it* in school. But I just thought of something. Something horrible."

"What?" I whispered, my heart pounding as I glanced around worriedly. The cafeteria was so chaotic that no one could have overheard us.

"What if it's a trick?" Darcy whispered.

"Huh?"

"The e-mail. What if there *is* no missing sister? What if someone's just playing a prank on us?"

I frowned. "Why would they do that?"

"To waste our time. To watch us run in circles,

trying to solve the mystery just so they could laugh in our faces."

"Who would do something like that?" I said disgustedly. "Something so . . . hateful."

Darcy lifted a hand to shield her pointing finger. I followed the direction she was pointing. Hunter Fisk. He was charging out of the cafeteria, laughing his obnoxious laugh.

"Revenge for what you did to him in social studies?" I wondered out loud.

"The timing is right," Darcy said. "We gave the presentation. I . . . well . . . humiliated him in class. Then, later that afternoon, we got the e-mail."

Gosh. It made sense. But I didn't picture Hunter coming up with such an elaborate plan to get back at us. He was usually more direct, like shoving kids into lockers and knocking books out of their hands.

Or . . . maybe I just didn't *want* it to be him. Maybe I wanted it to be someone innocent who really did need our help. The mystery was exciting to me. It was challenging. An adventure. I'd never really had an adventure before.

Either way, I wasn't ready to give up yet.

"I don't think we should assume it's Hunter," I said. "I don't want to quit. I want to keep investigating. But we'll keep our eyes on him. How's that?"

Darcy shrugged. "Works for me."

In gym class, we stood in formation as Mr. Edwards explained the rules of the volleyball match we were about to start. He always wore this whistle around his neck, even though I'd never seen him blow it. Not once.

I tried to pay attention to what Mr. Edwards was saying and not let my eyes drift to Zane. But he was wearing this really cool Reese's Peanut Butter Cups T-shirt. I wondered if that was his favorite candy.

Darcy whispered, "Will you stop daydreaming about Zane Munro and pay attention?"

I put my hands on my hips. "I am not daydreaming about —"

Mr. Edwards finished his talk and tossed a volleyball at me. I caught it in both hands and gazed around in confusion. Everyone looked at me like they were expecting me to do something. *Whoops.* I guessed I should have been paying attention.

This probably wouldn't help with my "being picked last" problem.

After a few moments of frozen silence, Fiona nudged me with her elbow. "You have to serve it."

Like food? I looked at her in bewilderment. I really should have listened to Mr. Edwards!

"You're in the server spot." Fiona mimicked hitting the ball with her hand.

Oh! I was in the last row, all the way to the right. Apparently, the person in this position had to hit the ball first.

Okay, I thought. *Here goes nothing.*

I hit the ball overhand with my open palm. Instead of flying over the net, it hit Maya Doshi in the shoulder, two rows in front of me.

"Ouch!" She turned around, rubbing her shoulder.

Hunter and Slade burst out laughing, pointing at Maya.

"It's not funny!" I said. "Sorry, Maya."

She nodded at me but didn't say anything.

"Make a fist," Fiona said. "And hit it underhand."

I closed my hand and focused on putting all my power into my fist. I reared my hand back and brought it forward, launching the volleyball high over the net to the other side. It dropped between two kids who weren't paying attention (probably not expecting my serve to actually make it over there). And my team got a point! I clapped excitedly.

I didn't know what was weirder: that Fiona had actually been helpful to me or that I'd finally found a sport I wasn't terrible at.

I was sad when it wasn't my turn to serve anymore, but the other positions were fun, too. Especially the front row, where you can jump up high and try to spike it onto the other side. I did that two times! For once, being the tallest girl in my grade was kind of cool. Everyone on the team gave me high fives (except Slade Durkin, but who cared about him?).

Usually, I watched the clock in gym class, begging time to go faster. But when I looked up and saw that there were only five minutes left, I was disappointed. The game was nearly over and we only needed one more point to win. Darcy and I were in the middle row. Slade was in front, which was good because he was our tallest player.

The other team served, and it sailed to our back row, where Maya stood, wide-eyed. She tried to hit the ball back but ended up giving it a light tap.

Oh no! I thought. I'd really wanted to win.

But then I saw that the ball was right above Slade, in perfect spiking position. He would have no problem smashing it down on the other side of the net. Probably too fast for their front row to return it.

But instead, Slade twisted to the side. He spiked the ball, all right.

Into Darcy's face.

She fell to the ground, covering her face with her hands.

"Slade!" Mr. Edwards yelled. "What was that?"

"I'm sorry, Mr. Edwards," he said. "I don't know what happened. I must have gotten turned around when I jumped up so high. It's too bad Maya couldn't hit it over the net."

"Oh, like this is her fault," I snapped. "You did that on purpose!"

He pretended to be shocked and put his hand to his chest. "I did not. I'm sorry Darcy got hurt, but that happens in sports. She should have been paying better attention."

The bell rang and Mr. Edwards dismissed everyone, clearly buying Slade's story. I knelt beside Darcy and pulled her hands down. I was expecting a bloody nose, but her face was just bright red.

"Are you okay?" I asked, and she nodded.

I couldn't believe she wasn't crying. I would have been bawling.

"Norah," Mr. Edwards said. "Please bring Darcy to the nurse to get her checked out."

Slade put his hand out, offering to help Darcy up. She looked at him with narrowed eyes, but took his hand.

He pulled her to her feet, then leaned closer and whispered, "That's for Hunter."

Chapter 6

All Darcy needed, according to the school nurse, was five minutes with an ice pack. So I sat next to my BFF on the vinyl couch in the nurse's office and tried not to think about how many kids had probably barfed in there.

I tried to focus on poor Darcy. She sat scowling with an ice pack on her nose. "I'd better not swell up," she groaned.

"Let me see," I said.

Darcy pulled the bag away. Her skin was a little puffy around her nose and it was bright red, but that would fade soon. It didn't look like she would be left with a bruise.

"It looks fine," I said, trying to soothe her.

Darcy squeezed the ice pack between her hands, and I had the feeling she was imagining it was Slade Durkin's neck. "Slade did that on purpose."

"I know," I said.

Darcy gazed up at me, one eyebrow raised. "Maybe *he's* the one who sent us the e-mails."

It was starting to seem like Darcy pointed the finger at whoever she was most angry with at that moment.

Probably seeing the doubt on my face, Darcy added, "You heard what he whispered. He did that for Hunter, his best friend. And, while Hunter probably isn't smart enough to think of a revenge plan like using our website, Slade *would* think of that. He's more . . . diabolical."

I rolled my eyes. "Jeez, Darcy, he's not a demon."

"Still," she continued, "think about it. Hunter and Slade. It could be them. Working together. Trying to get us to run around and solve a case that doesn't exist. It's just something they made up."

"Well, there's only one way to find out," I said. "Let's continue with our plan and figure out if anyone in our class has April fourth as their birthday."

"And if they don't?"

"Then . . . maybe you're right and it was only a joke."

I really hoped that wasn't the case. Not because I was scared of Slade or Hunter making fun of us for believing a fake e-mail. But because I didn't want all this excitement to be for nothing. Just the idea of that depressed me.

Darcy was feeling better, so we left the nurse's office. It was right next to the principal's office, so we waved to the school secretary and told her we were heading back to class. We were halfway down the empty hallway when I stopped Darcy in her tracks.

"Okay," I whispered. "We can't wait until after school to talk about this. We have to strategize now."

I heard a sound, like a shoe scuffing on the floor. We both looked back and forth, but the hallway was still empty.

"Maybe we should split the class list in two," I said. "I take half, you take half. And, over the course of the week, we ask every person what their birthday is and write it down."

Darcy grimaced. "Doesn't that seem kind of . . . weird? I mean, some of them are going to want to know why."

48

I rubbed my arm. "You're right. We need a cover story. But what reason could we possibly have for needing a list of everyone's birthdays?"

The noise came again, shoes shuffling on the floor. And then the door to the boys' bathroom opened and Zane stepped out.

He smiled. "I can help."

I suddenly forgot how to speak.

Fortunately, Zane didn't have the same effect on Darcy. She snapped, "Were you eavesdropping on us?"

"Not on purpose," Zane said. A little blush colored his cheeks. "I was in the bathroom and you guys were just, like, talking right outside of it."

"So you *were* listening to us," Darcy retorted.

I thought back over everything we'd said. Zane couldn't have heard anything *too* bad. Only that we needed our classmates' birthdays. Nothing about the missing twin. Finally, my throat loosened up and I could speak. "Stop giving him a hard time, Darcy. He offered to help."

As if suddenly remembering those were Zane's first words after stepping into the hallway, Darcy's eyes lit up. "How much did you hear?" she asked. "How exactly can you help?"

49

"Well," he said, stepping closer to us and lowering his voice, "I heard you two saying you need a list of our classmates' birthdays. And that you didn't want to go around asking one by one. So . . . I can get that for you."

Darcy narrowed her eyes doubtfully. "How?"

He shifted his weight back and forth. "I'm head of the seventh-grade student council. I can pass out a form and ask everyone to write their name and birth date. I'll tell them it's for a student council project."

My spirits lifted. What a great idea! They'd all believe that. And Darcy and I wouldn't have to go through the horror of asking each kid and deflecting their questions.

"And you won't tell anyone it's for us?" Darcy asked.

"Of course he won't," I piped up. Darcy was always so suspicious of people.

But, then again, she'd probably say I was too trusting.

Chapter 7

I made plans to meet Zane after school on Thursday.

I repeat . . . I made plans to meet ZANE.

Sorry, I just like saying those words.

Anyway, we chose Thursday afternoon so Zane would have a couple of days to get the "student council form" passed around. Zane and I decided to meet after school for the handoff. It was all so intriguing and fun. I felt like an international spy meeting a secret agent.

The school was emptying out, with kids heading toward buses and cars. Darcy and I took the bus together through elementary school. But once we entered seventh grade, we started going here, Danville Middle School, which is only a couple streets away from our houses. So we don't qualify for the bus anymore. Our moms drop us off in the mornings, but in the afternoons we walk home together.

Except today. I told Darcy I'd meet her back at her house after I got the paper from Zane. Part of me might've even been hoping he'd offer to walk me home. I rubbed my sweaty palms on my jeans as I waited.

Zane came around a corner and smiled when he saw me. My heart was thudding so loudly I wondered if he could hear it.

"Hey, Zane," I said in what I hoped was a casual voice. Then I added in a whisper, "Did you get it?"

He patted his backpack. "Yep!" His eyes were bright and excited, like he was keyed up for his part in the adventure. "This whole thing is so mysterious. I feel like I should've given you a secret signal."

I laughed. "Like they do in the movies!"

"Yeah! Like . . . I'd run my fingers through my hair."

"But you do that a lot anyway," I said quickly. The words came out before I could stop them, and my eyes widened. Now he'd know that I'd noticed that he often ran his hands through his hair. He'd think I stared at him all day long! Ah! Ah!

Before I could go into full panic-attack mode, Zane

said, "Good point. The signal should be something I don't normally do, so I can't do it by accident."

"Yeah," I said, hoping I wasn't blushing too much. "How about you just rub your right ear?"

"Like this?" He brought his hand up to his ear and wiggled it a bit.

"Sure. That will work."

"Okay, then. That's our secret signal." He pointed at the exit. "Shall we?"

We started walking side by side in front of the school. The sun was out and its rays felt warm on my face. The identity of our mystery client was in Zane's backpack. And I was out here walking with him. Was he going to walk me all the way home? Could this day get any better?!

"Well," he said, stopping. He slid a bunch of folded-up papers out of his bag and handed them to me. "This has been fun."

I took the papers and smiled. "Thanks for your help on the case—um, I mean . . . thanks for . . . everything."

Fortunately, he didn't seem to notice my slipup. "No problem. But I've got to go. Someone's waiting for me." He aimed a thumb over his shoulder.

Oh, I thought with some disappointment. Was his mom picking him up?

I looked at where he was pointing, but it wasn't his mom standing there.

It was Maya Doshi. *They* were walking home together.

I let myself into Darcy's house and trudged up the stairs toward her room. Zane had been so nice and helpful. I'd really wanted him to have a crush on me. Though from the looks of it, he liked Maya. But I didn't want to think about that, so I pushed it to the back of my mind. We had more important things to focus on.

I entered Darcy's bedroom, and my eyes immediately went to the dead body on her TV. I seriously didn't know how she watches all those crime shows and then sleeps well at night. Darcy sat cross-legged on her bed, biting her thumbnail, entranced in what the TV detectives were saying. After noticing me, she sat up straight and said, "Did you get it?"

I thought about playing a trick on her and pretending that I didn't, but it was no use. My emotions are always written all over my face. She'd know I was acting. So I unzipped my bag and pulled the papers out victoriously.

Darcy pumped her arm. "Zane really came through?"

"Yeah, but I haven't looked at it yet. I wanted to wait so we could do it together."

I kicked off my shoes, sat next to her on the bed, and pulled my legs up. Darcy pressed a button on the remote, shutting the TV off. I unfolded the papers. There were four, so I passed two to Darcy and kept two for myself.

"Let's see who our mystery e-mailer is!" Darcy said.

I couldn't read fast enough. I willed my eyes to take in each line quicker. Of course it didn't help that some of the kids in our class had worse handwriting than Hubble. By the time I reached the bottom of my first page, my hands were shaking with anticipation.

I was halfway down the second page when Darcy groaned. I looked up to see what was wrong.

"Finished," she said sadly. "No one with that birthday in my stack."

I tried to swallow, but my throat felt like it was full of sand. What if no one had the birthday? Did that really mean it was all just a joke?

I blinked and returned my eyes to the last few lines. I wanted it over with now. I just wanted to know, one way or the other. My finger trailed down the right side of the paper as I read each line. Then I stopped.

April fourth. There was the right date, written in purple ink. I froze for a moment, unable to breathe, move, even blink. Then, my heart beating wildly, my finger trailed to the left column to search for the name. I gasped.

"What?" Darcy said, inching closer to me. "Did you find something?"

"Yeah." I gulped. "I know who sent us the e-mail."

I squinted and reread the line just to be sure. But there it was.

Fiona Fanning.

Chapter 8

WaS Fiona Fanning really our mystery client? The question ran through my mind as I tried to sleep that night. And the next morning as I got ready for school. And in the hallway as I hurried to Darcy's locker. Darcy was even more impatient than I was to talk to Fiona. She'd wanted to call her right then and there last night! But I knew this was a conversation we had to have with Fiona face-to-face.

Darcy closed her locker as she saw me coming. She wore her usual attire: black jeans, a black T-shirt, and a dozen black jelly bracelets on her left wrist. If I had to name her fashion style, I'd call it "hip funeral."

"Can we go over there now?" Darcy nodded toward the other end of the hall. I turned to look.

Fiona was putting on lip gloss in the mirror that hung on the back of her locker door. A small circle of friends surrounded her, chattering away. Fitting, I thought, like the sun at the center of the solar system, with all the other planets orbiting it.

My eyes took in Fiona's outfit. Today she wore a lavender blouse with a short gray skirt, and pink-and-white striped tights. I never would have thought to put those colors and patterns together, but it looked perfect on Fiona.

I glanced down at my jeans and tan sweater and felt so plain. I wish fashion were like math. You'd pick two things and just know they added up and fit into the formula correctly. But clothes aren't like that. If I tried to put together a creative outfit like Fiona's, I'd end up looking like a circus clown.

Yeah, Fiona wasn't smart in the way Darcy and I were. But other stuff, like clothes and boys and being popular, came easy to her. And those things were mysteries to me. I found myself feeling a little jealous.

"Come on," Darcy said, pulling on the sleeve of my sweater. "Let's go talk to her."

"Wait," I said, thinking quickly.

Darcy rolled her eyes. "What? Are you scared?"

Adrenaline *was* rushing through my body. I felt almost hyper, like that time I drank four Cokes at my birthday party. But I wasn't scared. I was excited. We were close to getting some answers. But we also had to have patience. This had to be done the right way.

"No," I said in a hushed voice. "I just think we need to meet with Fiona alone."

"Why?" Darcy's tone was impatient. "Let's just go over there. Her friends will probably leave so they don't catch our nerd cooties."

"They might *not* leave, though," I said. "Fiona obviously doesn't want the whole world knowing about her sister. She e-mailed us anonymously. So if we confront her right in front of her friends, she'll probably pretend she doesn't know what we're talking about."

Darcy hesitated, chewing her lip. "Yeah. You're right. We should wait." She let out a heavy sigh. "How are we going to get her alone, though?"

I'd just been thinking about that. "We could put a note in her locker, telling her to meet us somewhere during lunch."

"The auditorium's always empty at that time," Darcy suggested. "We could have her meet us behind the stage."

I nodded quickly. "Good idea." I thought for a moment. "The only problem is, what if she doesn't find the note until after lunch?"

A slow smile spread across Darcy's face. "I have a way to make sure she'll get the message right now." She pulled her cell phone from her pocket and started a text message.

"How do you have Fiona's number?" I asked.

"I have everyone's number," she said matter-of-factly.

I could've asked how, but I had a feeling this was one of those "I don't want to know" things.

A minute later, Darcy looked back up. "Done!"

I risked a glance over my shoulder, but Fiona and her friends were gone. "I wonder if she'll come."

"Oh, she'll come. I made sure of that." Darcy slipped her phone to me so I could read the sent message.

Fiona —
Meet me backstage during lunch. Come alone.
— Bailey

Chapter 9

It was dark behind the thick red stage curtain. The lights were off in the auditorium, and since it was cloudy out, only a bit of daylight was coming through the windows. Enough for us to see our way around but too little to make out what most of the stuff in the crowded backstage area was.

Darcy sifted through a box of props and pulled out a sword made of rubber. She sliced it through the air and posed dramatically. "En garde!"

I took it from her and tossed it back in the box. "We don't have time to play. Let's figure out what we're going to say to Fiona."

Darcy said, "How about . . . 'Hey, we know you sent us that e-mail'?"

It seemed obvious, but I still wanted to prepare. I'm a planner; what can I say? "So we're going to just come right out with it?"

"That's how the TV detectives do it," Darcy said. "Direct confrontation. The element of surprise."

Suddenly, we heard one of the auditorium's metal double doors open and close. The sound was as loud as a truck crashing into a train.

"She's here," Darcy whispered.

I'd been so excited about this secret meeting all morning. But now my nerves were all jittery. I was glad I hadn't eaten my lunch beforehand, because my stomach was doing somersaults.

Darcy and I padded to the edge of the stage and peeked out from the corner, where the curtain meets the side wall. Fiona was walking slowly down the center aisle, her eyes darting around the room, her hands clasped in front of her. She reached the stage stairs and stopped. She tucked a strand of her high-lighted brown hair behind her ear.

She walked up the steps and paused again, taking a deep breath. Then she whipped open the curtain. She didn't immediately see us, because of the dim light and the fact that we were huddled in the corner, watching her.

After she let the curtain close behind her, she took a larger step into the backstage area and whispered, "I'm here."

Darcy and I stepped out of the shadows. Darcy said, "So are we."

Fiona stared at us. We stared at her. No one said anything for a moment.

"Did you send me the text message?" she asked, more to Darcy than me.

"Did you send us the e-mail?" I said in response.

Fiona shifted back and forth, studying her shoes. After a moment of deep thought, she let out a long breath and looked back up at us. "How did you find .out it was me?"

Darcy opened her mouth to speak, but I quickly said, "Don't worry about that." I didn't know what Darcy was going to say and I wanted to keep Zane's involvement out of it. "So, is what you said in your e-mail true?" I asked.

Fiona nodded slowly. "Yes. Bailey is my twin sister. And I need you to find her for me."

Getting the e-mail was one thing, but hearing the words come out of Fiona's mouth sent ripples of goose bumps up my arms.

"Was she kidnapped or something?" Darcy said.

Fiona shook her head and shrugged at the same time. "That's the thing. I don't know."

"Why don't you start at the beginning," I said.

Fiona fiddled with her jangly gold bracelets. "One day a couple weeks ago, I went searching through my parents' files. I was just looking for my Social Security number. I wanted to try to get a credit card because my allowance isn't enough and my parents don't understand the price of looking good."

Darcy opened her mouth, probably ready with a snarky remark. And, of course, I wanted to tell Fiona that you had to be eighteen to get a credit card. And that it's not magic money. She'd still have to pay for everything she charged. But the lesson in personal finance could wait. As could Darcy's comment. So I gave Darcy a stern look. She kept quiet and Fiona continued.

"But instead of finding my Social Security card, I found something that made no sense."

"What?" I asked. If I'd been sitting down, I would have been literally on the edge of my seat.

"A birth certificate with my birthday, but a different girl's name."

I shivered as a chill trailed down my spine.

"What makes you think she's your twin?" Darcy asked.

"Because *my* birth certificate was right next to it. Bailey Banks and Fiona Fanning. Born in the same city, at the same hospital, on the same day."

"But why would Bailey have a different last name from yours?" I said.

Fiona shook her head. "I don't know. But her being my twin is the only thing that makes sense. Why else would my parents have her birth certificate, right with mine? Plus, there's something else."

"What?" Darcy and I said at the same time.

"I found baby pictures. Two of them. They're those typical newborn pictures that are taken in the hospital, you know? They're definitely different babies, because one has a little pink onesie and the other has a purple one. But they look exactly alike."

"Twins," I said. Fiona was right. It was the only

thing that made sense. "Have you asked your parents?"

"No." Fiona's voice turned sad. "I feel betrayed by them. Whatever this secret is, they've kept it from me all my life. I don't trust them to tell me the truth." She looked up at us with glassy eyes. "I need to know what happened to her. Was she given up for adoption? Did something happen, but I was too young to remember it? Was she kidnapped? I need to know."

"I understand," I said softly. I couldn't imagine what she was going through. Wondering if your twin was out there somewhere or if something horrible had happened to her. She deserved to know the truth.

"I wouldn't even know how to start looking into it myself," Fiona said. "That's why I e-mailed you guys. You're, like, the smartest girls in school. If anyone could figure this out, it'd be you." She paused. "Will you help me?"

She looked so desperate, appealing to us for help. There was no way I could turn her down. And, without even looking at her face, I knew Darcy was in. If you wanted to get on her good side, call her the smartest girl in school. It worked like calling most girls pretty.

I was about to say that we'd help her when Darcy quickly said, "Have you thought that things could be the other way around?"

Fiona raised an eyebrow. "What do you mean?"

"That *you* were the one who was adopted or kidnapped."

I expected some sort of reaction from Fiona, but not an invitation.

"Come over to my house after school," she said calmly. "You'll see."

Chapter 10

OF course "after school" for Fiona meant four o'clock because she had cheering practice first. But I didn't mind waiting. I walked Hubble and finished all my homework in my room. When it was nearly four o'clock, I came back downstairs. Hubble was asleep on his back in his doggie bed, lightly snoring. Mom was chopping vegetables in the kitchen.

"I'm heading over to Fiona's with Darcy now," I said, pointing at the door. "We're riding our bikes there. Okay?"

I expected a quick nod and a reminder to be home for dinner, but Mom stopped chopping, wiped her hands on a dish towel, and turned around.

"Why are you hanging out with Fiona Fanning?" Mom asked. "She doesn't seem like a girl you'd be friends with." In addition to curiosity, I sensed happiness in Mom's voice. Like maybe she was hoping some of Fiona would rub off on me.

"Darcy and I are helping her out with something. She's trying to find . . . herself," I invented at the last minute.

"Well," Mom said, smiling. "I'm glad you're all broadening your group of friends."

I nodded and was almost to the door when Mom added, "Be home for dinner. If you're going to be late, call so I don't worry."

"It *would* be easier for me to call if I had my own cell phone, you know," I said. I liked to remind my parents of this any time I could.

"Yeah, yeah," Mom said. "You can use the Fannings' phone. Or Darcy's."

Sigh. It had been worth a try.

By the time I got outside, Darcy was standing there leaning against her bike. She had a boys' bike, mainly because she hated all the colors the girl ones came in.

"I thought you'd never get out here," she said, tapping her foot.

"My mom was wondering why we're suddenly friends with Fiona," I explained. "But it's cool. Let's go."

We hopped on our bikes.

It was a beautiful fall afternoon. The air was crisp but not chilly enough that you'd need a coat. I'm not one of those kids who enjoys riding my bike. I mainly use it to get from point A to point B. But I had to admit that today, with the wind in my hair and the sun on my face, it was a nice feeling.

Before I knew it, we were at Fiona's address. The house was typical from the outside, white with beige trim. It kind of reminded me of a box. Though I imagined that the inside would be decorated like one of those fancy house magazines you look at when you're stuck waiting for your dad at Home Depot.

We left our bikes in the driveway and walked up to the door. Darcy pressed the doorbell. After, like, three seconds she pressed it again.

"Sheesh," I said. "Give her a minute."

Muffled footsteps rapidly approached, and then the door swung open.

I immediately knew why Fiona had invited us over.

Fiona answered the door, but not Fiona. It was an older Fiona. Still pretty, with that same long, high-lighted brown hair and big green eyes.

It was Fiona's mother. And Fiona was definitely not adopted.

Mrs. Fanning didn't exactly give us a welcoming smile. She looked confused.

"Um," Darcy said. "We're here to see Fiona?" It sounded like a question.

Fiona came dashing around the corner and skidded to a stop. "Hey, guys," she said to us with a little wave. To her mother, she said, "This is Norah and Darcy."

Mrs. Fanning frowned. "You didn't tell me you'd invited friends over."

"They're not staying for dinner, so I figured you didn't need to know."

"Fiona," Mrs. Fanning said in a low voice. "We've been through this. You know our house rule."

Wow. And I thought *my* parents were strict.

"Yeah, yeah, Mom." Fiona rolled her eyes. "Lecture me later."

I didn't know if they were going to argue in front of us or what. Mrs. Fanning was definitely considering it. But she apparently decided to be polite, because she smiled and opened the door wide. "Please come in, girls."

The inside of the house was nothing like I'd imagined. As Fiona led us through the entry, past the living room, and into the kitchen, I noticed that all the walls were the same off-white color. The framed art on the walls was generic, like the pictures that come with the frame. Every room was just so . . . ordinary.

Her mother followed us into the kitchen and started flipping through a book. I assumed it was a cookbook, but she was scribbling in it with a pencil.

"We're going to grab some snacks to bring up to my room," Fiona said.

Mrs. Fanning looked us over. I felt like she was judging us in some way, and I didn't like it. Yeah, I didn't have cool clothes like Fiona and we definitely weren't part of the popular crowd, but that didn't mean we were unworthy to be in her house.

"Do you go to Danville Middle School?" Mrs. Fanning asked us.

"Yep," Darcy said.

I nodded.

Finoa passed us each a can of soda, grabbed a large bag of chips, and pushed us forward with her arms. "Let's head to my room."

Upstairs, Fiona closed the door behind us and tossed the snacks on her bed.

Walking into Fiona's room was like entering fairy princess land. Everything was pink and glittery. I half expected a unicorn to walk out of her closet.

I must have been staring, because Fiona said, "Isn't it great? This is the only room in the house with any taste."

"Yeah," Darcy said sarcastically. "It's . . . great."

The bright colors and girly furniture were Darcy's worst nightmare.

There was a light knock on the door. It sounded like a code. Rap . . . rap rap . . . rap rap rap.

Fiona smiled and opened the door.

A little girl waddled in, clutching a stuffed penguin in her arms. As much as Mrs. Fanning looked like an older version of Fiona, this girl was the mini version.

"Hi!" the girl said to us.

Darcy and I waved.

"This is my little sister, Mia," Fiona said in a sweet,

high voice. That definitely wasn't a tone she used at school.

"Can we play?" Mia asked.

Fiona bent down. "I'm super busy right now, but I will definitely play with you after dinner. Okay?"

Mia nodded happily and skipped away. Fiona shut the door behind her.

I'd expected Fiona to roll her eyes and dismiss her sister as annoying. But she didn't. At school, Fiona could be mean and insulting to kids who weren't popular. But here she was, being super nice to her little sister. I couldn't quite figure her out.

"So," Fiona said, opening a bag of chips, "now you know why I'm sure I'm not adopted."

Fiona sat on the rug. We joined her and she passed the bag of chips around.

"Yeah, you're a clone of your mom," Darcy said.

"Only on the surface," Fiona corrected. "We look alike, but we are nothing alike. My mom doesn't know anything about fashion or style. She spends all her time cooking and cleaning and doing her stupid puzzle books. Dad's either working or reading technology magazines." She shook her head in disgust. "They are such dorks."

"What does your dad do for work?" I asked, reaching into the bag for a chip. They were salt and vinegar flavored, my favorite.

"He works for a computer company. And when he's at home, he reads about computers." She rolled her eyes. "They are so lame. I don't know where *I* came from."

Darcy rubbed her chin. "So you're not adopted, that's clear. But maybe Bailey was. Do you have those baby pictures?"

Fiona went to her desk, which was covered with various bottles of lotion and nail polish, slid open a drawer, and took out two photos. She handed the pictures to us, and Darcy and I studied them.

Most babies kind of look alike to me anyway, but these two were almost exact. They both had small pale faces with the same little button noses. And they had an equal amount of light brown fuzz on the tops of their heads. The only real difference I could see was in their outfits and the fact that one baby's head was turned slightly more to the left than the other. They *could* be twins.

"And can we see the birth certificates?" I asked.

Fiona pulled two pieces of paper out of her desk.

Darcy took one and I took the other. We compared them side by side. Bailey's certificate was faded in spots, like it was a photocopy, not an original. Some lines were clear.

CHILD'S NAME (FIRST MIDDLE LAST):
   Bailey Ann Banks
GENDER: Female
DATE OF BIRTH: April 4
PLACE OF BIRTH: Garretson, SD

All of that, except the name, was the same as the certificate for Fiona Erin Fanning. Maura and Roger Fanning were listed as the parents on Fiona's paper. On Bailey's, the lines containing the parents' names were too faded to read.

"Do you remember living in Garretson, South Dakota?" I asked Fiona.

Fiona shook her head. "I've never even heard of the place. I always assumed I was born here, in Massachusetts."

"Fiona!" Mrs. Fanning called from downstairs. "Dinner will be ready soon!"

I think that was a polite way of kicking Darcy and me out.

Fiona let out a sigh that sounded so sad. It was strange to see her vulnerable like this.

On our way out, we were stopped at the foot of the stairs by a bellowing voice. "Fiona! Aren't you going to introduce your friends?"

Fiona groaned and pointed toward the den. "Dad's home from work," she whispered. "This will only take a minute."

We followed her into the room. Built-in bookcases lined the walls and were crammed with books from floor to ceiling. A desk had a pile of puzzle workbooks with titles like *World's Hardest Crosswords* and *Impossible Sudoku*.

In short, my kind of room.

Mrs. Fanning was sitting in a recliner with a pencil in one hand. In the other she had a book called *Mind Benders*. She sure liked puzzles. Mr. Fanning was in a matching chair, reading *PC Magazine*. He looked at us over the rim of his glasses. "Who are your friends, honey?" he asked, and, like Mrs. Fanning, he had a note of suspicion in his tone.

"Norah Burridge and Darcy Carter," Fiona said impatiently. "They go to my school. But they have to head home now."

Fiona led us outside and walked us down the driveway to our bikes.

"Why didn't you tell your parents that we were coming over?" Darcy asked.

Fiona waved her hands in the air dramatically. "Because they would have made a huge deal out of it and asked twenty questions about each of you. My parents are so totally overprotective. They always have to know who I'm meeting, where I'm going, what time I'll be back, who all the kids' parents are, blah, blah, blah. If this continues into high school, I'm never going to have a real social life."

I tried not to roll my eyes as I lifted my bike's kickstand with my foot. I didn't feel like we were any closer to giving Fiona her answers, but I wanted to leave on a positive note. "Well, thanks for having us over," I said. "We learned a *little* bit more."

"Not really." Fiona put her face in her hands and groaned. "How will I ever find out the truth?" she asked, her voice breaking a little.

I'd already decided I was going to help her, but I looked at Darcy. She nodded once and I knew we agreed.

"We'll do it," Darcy said.

Fiona looked up with hope in her glistening eyes. "You'll help me find Bailey?"

I placed a gentle hand on Fiona's shoulder. "Sure. We'll help you."

We all stood awkwardly for a moment. I didn't know what we should do. Hug? We still weren't exactly friends. Shake hands? That seemed too . . . professional.

Darcy held her fist out. "Bump it," she said.

I bumped first and Fiona followed my lead with a grin.

Chapter 11

We weren't going to see Fiona again until Monday, but that wouldn't stop Darcy and me from investigating. We made plans to meet at Darcy's house Saturday for some Internet research. My house was out of the question since our computer is in the living room, and my parents would be staring over our shoulders the whole time. Then they'd want to know what we were doing and I'd be faced with the choice of either (a) telling them we're investigating a real missing person case (after which they'd freak out and decide it was too dangerous) or (b) lying to them (after which I'd feel so guilty I'd have a stomachache for days).

So doing the work at Darcy's would avoid all that unnecessary drama.

I woke up Saturday morning and ate a bowl of cereal while watching TV — something I wasn't allowed to do on school days. I had about ten minutes before I had to be at Darcy's, so I decided to take Hubble for a walk. Mom and Dad were snuggled on the couch, sharing the newspaper, and I waved 'bye to them.

After I'd clipped on his leash, Hubble pulled me down the driveway and to the sidewalk. "Hey, who's walking who here?" I said.

Yes, I talk to my dog. What of it?

He stopped at the fire hydrant in front of our house and sniffed circles around it for a couple minutes. I sighed and waited.

Finally, I said, "Listen, Hubble. *You* know you're going to pee on the hydrant. *I* know you're going to pee on the hydrant. You pee on that thing every day. Stop acting like you're trying to make a decision and just do it."

He looked up at me, head tilted to the side, then lifted his leg and got down to business.

"Thank you," I whispered.

After he'd finished, he suddenly got excited and started to do his head-to-tail-wiggle dance. Which meant only one thing. Darcy was here.

I turned around and saw her stomping up the sidewalk toward me.

I looked at my watch. "I'm not late!" I said. "I have two more minutes."

"Plans have changed," she said, kneeling down to pet Hubble, who was so excited he was trying to lick her face off.

"What's going on?" I asked.

She straightened and wiped her face with her sleeve. "The school called. Mom's mad. Long story short, my laptop and phone have been confiscated for the weekend."

I groaned. "Can't you go one week without getting in trouble?"

"Hey, he started it. And you didn't seem to mind that day when I was standing up for your dream boy."

"Wait, what?" I was so confused.

Darcy's shoulders sagged. "Hunter Fisk and his parents made a visit to the principal to complain about me tying his shoelace to his chair. They said I was bullying him."

My jaw dropped. "He's the bully, not you! *He* was torturing poor Zane." I was furious. Darcy was in trouble for only giving Hunter what he deserved, and he got away with his behavior. Again.

Hubble looked up at me warily. He could always sense my emotions.

"I'm going to call Principal Plati and tell him what really happened," I said in almost a yell. "We can ask Zane, too, and then —"

Darcy shook her head. "Don't bother. If Zane tattled, it would only make things worse for him. Plus, it's not like I got suspended or anything. Plati just called my mom." She shrugged. "Two days without technology. I'll live."

"But what about our investigation? We need your laptop."

"No biggie." She pointed at my house. "We'll use your computer."

I looked over my shoulder and back again. "Darcy . . . you know my parents have it in the living room so they can keep an eye on me. They'll want to know what we're doing and —"

Darcy smiled as she interrupted me. "Don't worry. I have an idea."

We came back into my house, and I unclipped Hubble's leash. He ran off, probably to find his favorite toy. We turned the corner into the living room, and my parents were still on the couch.

"Oh, hi, girls," Mom said, looking up from her section of the paper. "I thought you were going to Darcy's house today."

Darcy stuffed her hands in the pockets of her jeans and hung her head. "We were, but I asked Norah if it was okay if we met here instead. My mom's kind of overwhelmed today and I thought I should get out of her hair."

I looked at Darcy, wondering where this was coming from.

Mom's and Dad's faces grew concerned. "What's wrong with your mother?"

Darcy shook her head sadly. "You know, she just has so much to do. And it's stuff I can't help her with. Like today she wants to clean the gutters on the house. It's just . . . it's a lot."

Dad straightened. "Can we help her?"

Mom nodded quickly. "We'd love to help out. It's a beautiful day to do outside work."

"I don't know." Darcy shuffled her feet back and forth. "She sure could use the help, but she would never ask. And she'd be real mad at me if she knew I told you."

"Here's what we'll do," Mom said, standing. "We'll pretend we're going for a nice walk and then insist on helping her. She'll never know you told us."

Darcy looked at me. I tried my best to keep my expression flat.

"That would be wonderful, Mr. and Mrs. Burridge!" she said.

And, within minutes, my parents were out the door.

I had to hand it to her. Darcy knew how to play my parents. They had a soft spot for Darcy's mom and respected her for "trying so hard to raise a difficult girl as a single mother." So anytime they saw an opportunity to help her out, they jumped at the chance.

"Well," I said, looking at my parents' old desktop, "we have unsupervised computer use now."

"But only for an hour," Darcy pointed out. "With the three of them cleaning those gutters, it won't take long."

I pressed the button on the computer, turning it on. "Then let's get started."

Darcy tapped her black-painted fingernails on the keyboard tray while we waited for the computer to boot up. "When did your parents buy this? The ice age?"

I sighed. "I told you it was old. My parents aren't very tech-savvy. As long as it still works, they won't buy a new one."

The hard drive groaned and whirred. Darcy leaned forward and peered through the vents on the side.

"What are you looking for?" I asked.

"The hamster that powers this thing. Where's his wheel?"

I groaned. I was getting sick of Darcy's jokes. Finally, the monitor flickered to life, and welcome noises came from the speakers.

"Okay," I said, offering up the keyboard to her. "Where should we start?"

Darcy settled into the chair while I stood beside it. "Let's start with a simple search engine lookup of her name."

Darcy's fingers hammered at the keyboard. I didn't know how she could type so fast. Entries for *Bailey Ann Banks* popped up on the screen.

We scanned them for a while, clicking on a few from social networks. Finally, I said with disappointment, "These girls are all too old to be our Bailey."

"Yeah, I figured she would be too young to have an online page," Darcy said. "But it was worth a try."

I glanced out the window, wondering how far along the gutter cleaning had come. We'd wasted too much time on these wrong Baileys. "So now what?"

Darcy clicked the mouse and brought us to a website I'd never seen before. "Now we try the database."

"What's that?" I asked.

"It's just this website I have a subscription to. You enter personal information like names and ages and track people down. You can even get background reports and phone numbers."

I had the feeling that Darcy had done this before. Hence, the subscription. I put my hands on my hips and gave her The Look.

"What?" Darcy said innocently. "My mom went on a date last year with this guy I didn't like. So I got access to this website so I could look into his background. Believe me, I saved her some trouble."

I couldn't help but laugh. It was hard to be annoyed with Darcy's behavior when she did it out of protective feelings for her mom. Plus, it was coming in handy today.

"So it's really this easy?" I said. "We type in *Bailey Ann Banks* and we could have her phone number in a minute?"

"Well, it will take a bit longer because most entries don't include a middle name," Darcy explained, typing away. "So we have to look through all the Bailey Bankses. We can start here in Massachusetts or in South Dakota, where she was born. But she could be anywhere, so we may have to widen the search."

Soon a list of Bailey Bankses came up on the screen. More than I would have liked. "That's a lot of Bailey Bankses."

"It's okay," Darcy said. "We can immediately skip the ones with a middle name or initial other than A. We'll focus on Bailey Banks, Bailey Ann Banks, and Bailey A. Banks."

I nervously looked at my watch. "When do you think my parents will be back?"

Darcy leaned forward, closer to the monitor, with a determined look on her face. "You go spy out the window and see how much progress they've made. I'll start looking for our Bailey."

I jogged to the dining room to play lookout. The window in that room faced Darcy's house. I peeked out and — surprisingly — didn't see anyone. The ladder was on the grass . . . as if they had already finished. I gasped and ran back to Darcy.

"They're done! The ladder is back on the ground!" I said, panting.

Darcy was tracing her finger down the computer monitor and clicking around with the mouse. "Chill. They probably went in my house for some lemonade or something. My mom wouldn't let them go that easily. She likes to talk their ears off."

"Did you find her?" I asked, pointing at the screen.

"No." She sighed. "There's no Bailey Banks, age twelve, in the whole state of Massachusetts or South Dakota."

I groaned. "So what now?"

"I have to examine every twelve-year-old Bailey Banks in the entire country and see if I can narrow the list down at all."

That seemed like a big job. "I'll go to the front of the house and watch for them," I said, hoping Darcy wouldn't take too long.

But as I got near our front window, a shadow passed by. They were coming back!

I ran into the living room and whisper-screamed, "They're back! They're back!"

"Oh no!" Darcy rubbed her face. "I need more time."

"We'll just have to quit for now," I said. "Try again another day."

"No." Darcy bent down and flipped the switch to turn the printer on. "Stall them."

My eyes widened. "I can't!"

"Just for one minute," Darcy said as the printer whirred to life.

Thinking quickly, I darted to the front door and tore it open. My parents stood there openmouthed in surprise.

"We were just coming in, honey," Mom said.

"Have you seen Hubble?" I didn't even have to fake the panicked tone of my voice. I *was* panicking.

"No," Dad said, his brow creasing. "Did he get out?"

"I think so. I can't find him!" I stepped outside and closed the door behind me. Mom, Dad, and I wandered around the yard, calling out, "Hubble! Hubble!"

I looked under bushes and behind trees.

Dad said, "It's very strange. We've been outside working on Ms. Carter's gutters. We would have seen him running around if he'd gotten loose."

"Hubble!" Mom cried out, louder this time.

And he "woofed" in response.

We all turned around slowly, facing the house. And there was Hubble's little brown face in the window. He must have climbed onto the back of the sofa to peer outside and see what all the fuss was about. And, in doing so, he just may have gotten me busted.

Mom and Dad looked at me.

I opened my mouth, ready to spill everything.

And the front door flew open.

"I found him!" Darcy said, stepping outside. "We thought he'd gotten out because he wasn't coming when we called in the house. But it turns out he'd somehow gotten himself locked in the bathroom."

"Oh," Mom said. "Maybe the wind closed the door on him."

"Yeah, maybe," Darcy said, nodding. "Anyway, thanks so much for helping my mom. I bet she's in a better mood now. Let's go, Norah."

Darcy grabbed my hand and led me down the sidewalk.

"Be home in time for dinner," Mom called to my back, and I waved in response. Mom was making lasagna tonight, so I was actually looking forward to that.

But first . . . I wanted to see what Darcy had found.

We ran upstairs to Darcy's room, and she closed the door.

I looked at her empty hands. "You couldn't get the list to print?"

She smiled and reached under her purple-and-black striped T-shirt, then whipped out the paper and waved it in the air triumphantly. She'd stuffed the printout in the waistband of her jeans.

"Brilliant! Let's see it," I said eagerly.

"There are six pages of names." Darcy flipped through the papers. "Let's split it up and see what we find."

She handed me three pages. We both sat cross-legged on her bed and started reading.

Bailey K. Banks . . . I mentally crossed her off for having the wrong middle initial.

Bailey Banks, no middle name, in Kansas. I checked her age: forty-four. Nope.

I traced my finger down the page to the next entry. There was a Bailey A. Banks! My heart raced, thinking I might have found her. But it sank again as I saw she was twenty years old.

I continued down the list until the end, then looked up to find that Darcy had finished first. From the sour look on her face, I guessed she had come up empty-handed, too.

"Any luck?" I said, trying to force positivity into my voice.

"Nope. You?"

I shook my head.

"I don't get it," I said. "How could she not be anywhere in the country?"

Darcy picked at her fingernail polish and stared at the wall. "It's like Bailey Ann Banks doesn't exist."

Chapter 12

On Monday, even though we were in the middle of the most exciting project of our lives, everything seemed back to normal. Fiona ignored us in front of her friends. Hunter and Slade snickered at us as we walked by them in the hall. Zane wore a T-shirt with some band on it I didn't know and looked really cute. I got a 98 on a history test I had freaked out over. (I thought I had missed more than one question and had nearly given myself an ulcer worrying about it.) Darcy got a 96, with much less angst involved.

Darcy and I sat together at lunch. The cafeteria smelled like hot dogs. Not the good barbeque-grilled-hot-dogs-in-the-summer kind of smell. Steamed hot dogs. Barf.

"I've been thinking," she said.

I should have suspected something was going on in that brain of hers. Darcy had scarfed down her entire lunch in the time it took me to unwrap my sandwich. That was normal. But she'd stayed quiet in the minutes after. Now, *that* was unusual.

"I don't trust her," Darcy said.

I immediately knew who she was talking about. I turned to see Fiona sitting at the popular table, giggling with her friends.

"Why not?" I asked.

"Did you watch her in class today?" Darcy said, still looking at Fiona. "She was scribbling in a notebook the entire time."

"Taking notes, you mean?"

Darcy shook her head. "No, even when the teacher wasn't talking, she was scribbling. She definitely wasn't paying attention. She was doing something else."

"Do you mean that pink notebook she carries around with her everywhere?" I asked, and took a bite of my sandwich.

Darcy pointed at me. "Yes! And the fact that it's with her almost all the time. It makes me suspicious."

Now my wheels were turning. "What do you think it could be?"

Darcy's already dark eyes darkened further. "Maybe a slam book."

"What's that?"

"Something you write rumors and gossip in. Mean stuff about other kids."

"That sounds terrible." I dropped the remains of the sandwich back in the paper bag. I don't do crusts. "But what does that have to do with our investigation?"

"What if it's all a prank?" Darcy suggested. "What if Fiona, Hunter, Slade, all the popular kids are in on it? They sent us the e-mail and are making us go through this whole investigation for nothing. And she's making fun of us in that notebook."

Darcy sometimes sees conspiracies where there aren't any. She can get a bit paranoid. When she'd first brought up the idea of it all being a trick, I'd thought there was a possibility. But now we'd come so far. We'd matched Fiona's birthday. We'd seen actual evidence. "What about the birth certificate?" I asked.

Darcy thought for a minute. "It could have been faked. It was kind of faded."

"I doubt that," I said. Faking an official document seemed like way too much trouble to go through just to mess with us.

"Plus, she wasn't in the database," Darcy said. "The bottom line is we need to see what's in that notebook. We need to be sure."

I gazed over my shoulder at Fiona. She threw her head back in laughter at something one of her friends said. She was so confident. So put together. And, yeah, she could act like a mean girl sometimes. But Friday, when she was nearly in tears asking us for help . . . that couldn't have been an act.

Could it?

AFTER the final bell rang, I grabbed my jacket from my locker and headed outside to walk home with Darcy. It was one of those days that had started off cool in the morning, but now the afternoon sun had warmed the air up. I didn't need my jacket, so I stopped to tie it around my waist.

"Hold on a second," I said.

Darcy waited while I fumbled with the jacket arms. After a minute, I was ready. "Okay, let's go."

But someone came up behind us and said in a bubbly voice, "So whose house are we going to today?"

Darcy and I turned around slowly to face Fiona.

"For what?" Darcy snapped.

"To talk clues, of course," Fiona whispered. "I want to work *with* you guys and find out what you're learning as we go. Plus, I don't have cheering today."

"So we're not cool enough to talk to during the school day, but we're good enough to do all this work for you?" Darcy crossed her arms and made her angry face. It was only slightly different from her normal face.

Fiona looked at me — the nicer one — for support, but I just shrugged. Darcy had a point.

"Listen," Fiona said. "I'm sorry if I hurt your feelings by not chatting with you guys at all today. But I figured we'd want to keep this whole thing secret until we know what's going on."

That made sense, but I could tell it wasn't enough for Darcy. Her eyes narrowed suspiciously.

"See? I even wore my pearls." Fiona pointed to the string of pearls that hung around her neck over her pink sweater. She grinned. "Like Nancy Drew!"

I couldn't help but soften. Only Fiona would match fashion to mysteries. "Okay, we can go to my house today," I offered. Working on the investigation *might* be easier with Fiona, since she could have more information that she hadn't even thought of yet.

Plus . . .

I motioned with my eyes at the pink notebook Fiona held clutched to her chest, then looked back at Darcy.

My best friend smiled. "Yeah, let's go to Norah's. It'll be fun."

Darcy had understood my look. At my house, we'd find a way to peek into Fiona's notebook and find out if her motives were for real . . .

. . . or not.

Chapter

13

At first it felt strange walking home with Fiona. For one, it was always just Darcy and me. So adding a third anytime would have felt a little unusual. The fact that our third wheel was Fiona Fanning made it überweird.

But after a while, it was okay. We talked about classes and how one of the lunch ladies was so nice and the other so evil (they'd been nicknamed Mrs. Angel and Mrs. Devil). And before we knew it, we were at my house.

I opened the door and called out, "Hey, Mom! I have friends over!"

A moment later, Mom came around the corner, and her eyes lit up. "Hi, girls!" she said excitedly.

"Hey, Mom," I said. "This is Fiona Fanning."

Fiona smiled sweetly and gave a little wave. "Nice to meet you, Mrs. Burridge."

"Oh, I know Fiona," Mom said. "You did great at that runway show fund-raiser the PTA held last year."

Of course Mom recognized Fiona. Everyone in town knew who she was. Pretty, popular girls tend to be memorable.

"I love your nails," Mom said, taking one of Fiona's hands. "Did you do this yourself?"

I hadn't even noticed, but Fiona's nails were painted a glittery pink (probably to match her sweater) with a little design in the middle of each one.

"Oh, I had them done at Stylish Nails in the center of town," Fiona said gleefully. "Didn't they do a great job?"

"They sure did," Mom said. "I've been meaning to try them sometime. Do they do pedicures, too?"

"Of course!"

Darcy and I shared an eye roll. I started to pull Fiona away. "Okay, nice chatting with you, Mom, but we're going to go upstairs and do our homework now."

"Oh, okay," Mom said. I sensed disappointment in her voice. As we started up the stairs, she yelled, "Let me know if you want any snacks!"

"I'm sorry about that," I whispered to Fiona.

She waved me off. "No problem. Your mom's really cool."

Once we got upstairs, I closed the door to my room behind us. I slipped my backpack off my shoulder and dropped it on the bed, then motioned for Darcy and Fiona to do the same. I assumed Fiona's special notebook was in her backpack. We'd have to find a way to take a look at some point.

"What's this?" Fiona pointed to my telescope. "Do you spy on your neighbors?"

"Of course not," I said. Darcy started laughing, since she *was* my neighbor. I explained, "It's a telescope for watching the skies. You know, stars, planets, moons. I'm really into astronomy."

"Oh, cool!" Fiona said. "I'm an Aries."

Darcy was really laughing now. I wanted to put my face in my hands, but instead I calmly said, "Horoscopes and stuff . . . that's astrology. Totally different."

Fiona frowned. "Oh." She seemed much less interested now.

Darcy flopped onto her usual beanbag chair and I settled into the other. Fiona just stood there. Then

I realized the problem. I only had two beanbag chairs. I'd never had more than one friend in my room before.

I slid off the chair. "Fiona, you can take this one. I'll sit on the rug."

Darcy shot me a disapproving look and I glared back.

Yeah, we didn't know yet if we could trust Fiona. But I was still going to be a polite host until we knew for sure.

"Okay, let's go over what we have," I said.

Darcy opened a notebook she'd been writing the case information in. She read out loud, "Bailey and Fiona were born on the same day, in the same hospital, in the same city. There were also two baby photos showing two different babies who looked almost exactly alike. The parents' names were too faded to read on Bailey's birth certificate, though, so we can't be sure Fiona and Bailey have the same parents. And then there's the question of why Bailey would have a different last name. But we know that Fiona wasn't adopted or kidnapped, because she looks exactly like her mother."

Fiona fiddled with her pearls. "Though if I was kidnapped, that would explain a lot." She said dreamily, "Maybe my real mother lives in New York City and works at *Vogue* and has spent her whole life mourning her daughter, who was kidnapped as an infant."

"Let's focus on the facts," I said. Just because Fiona's mom was nothing like her, that didn't mean she wasn't her mother. Case in point: my parents and me. Nothing in common. At all.

Darcy frowned, flipping a page in her notebook. "The strange thing is that, though Bailey exists on that birth certificate you found, she doesn't exist in the database."

"What do you mean?" Fiona asked, her forehead creasing.

I explained, "Darcy looked up all the Bailey Ann Bankses through this online website that private investigators use." *And people like Darcy*, I added silently. "There are no Baileys with that birth year born in South Dakota. Nothing that matches the birth certificate. It's like she doesn't exist."

"Or that her existence was wiped," Darcy said.

Thinking out loud, I asked, "But who would do that? And why?"

"Kidnappers!" Fiona said.

She really seemed to be sticking with that theory.

"Okay," I said. "So she's not in the secret database. Files can be deleted. Why don't we go to the source? Get the original birth certificate."

Darcy snapped her fingers. "That's a great idea, Norah!" She pulled out her smartphone and typed something in.

"What are you doing?" I asked.

"Getting the phone number for the city hall in Garretson, South Dakota," Darcy said.

A moment later, she put the phone in my hand.

"Me?" I yelled. My heart started thumping. "What am I supposed to say?"

Darcy said, "You're Bailey Banks and you need a copy of your original birth certificate."

An older woman's voice came on the line. "City Hall. This is Mary; how can I help you?"

My mouth opened, but nothing came out. Darcy made a spinning motion with her hand, signaling me to get talking. Fiona just sat there looking confused by the whole thing.

"Um, yes," I said, my voice finally working. "My name is Bailey Banks and I don't live in South Dakota anymore, but I was born there. My birth certificate is all faded and, um, messed up and I need a new one for . . . um . . . school."

"Ah, transferring, are you?" the woman said.

"Yes, I'm transferring to a new school," I replied.

Darcy nodded in approval at my act.

Mary said, "Okay, I can help you out." I heard her fingers clicking at a keyboard. "I'll need you to mail in — wait a minute."

She paused and I pushed the phone harder into my ear like that would help me see what was going on in the town hall right now.

"Well, that's strange," Mary said. More keyboard clicking.

"What is it?" I asked.

"Are you sure you were born in Garretson, dear?"

"Yes. That's what my birth certificate says."

"Well, we have no birth certificate on file for a Bailey Banks. . . ." The woman's voice trailed off, and I wondered if she thought I was pranking her.

"Maybe it's not in the computer, but the hard copy is still in the file?" I said. "You know . . . computers these days." I figured that was a statement an older woman could relate to.

She agreed with a little grunt. "Hold for a moment and I'll check."

I covered the phone with my hand and whispered to Darcy and Fiona, "I'm on hold."

"What's going on?" Fiona whispered back.

"She couldn't find Bailey Banks in the computer, so she's checking the actual files to see if a hard copy of the birth certificate is in there."

A few minutes later, the woman returned to the phone. "I'm sorry, darlin', but there's no paper original here either. You must have some bad information about where you were born."

I thanked her and hung up. Darcy and Fiona were basically panting like Hubble does when you hold a treat in front of his nose.

"What? What?" Darcy said.

"What did she say?" Fiona echoed.

I shrugged. "The city of Garretson, South Dakota, has no record of Bailey Banks being born." I nodded at Fiona. "I think the only evidence that Bailey ever existed is in your house."

They both groaned and leaned back in the beanbag chairs. I wasn't ready to give up, though. "Is there anywhere else we can look for proof that Bailey really existed?" I asked.

Darcy scratched her mop of hair. "The only other place to try would be the Social Security database, but that would be hard to get into. I'm not saying impossible, but —"

"Darcy," I interrupted. "Do not hack into a government website. We could end up in juvie."

Fiona gasped. "Do they make you wear those orange prison jumpsuits? Orange is my worst color."

"No one's going to prison," I said. "No one's hacking any websites. We're doing this legitimately. Fiona, have you found anything else in your house that seems suspicious at all?"

She thought for a moment, one hand clutching her pearls. "I haven't really searched since I found the birth certificates and the photos."

"So here's our next step," I said. "You search your house. Especially in any drawers or file cabinets your parents have. Like in the den. See if you can find any other evidence that Bailey is real."

I glanced at Darcy to see if she had anything else to add, but it was like she wasn't even listening anymore. She suddenly stood up, said, "I need a snack," and leaned over the bed where the back-packs were.

Fiona shrugged and looked back at me.

But I knew what Darcy was doing. That wasn't *her* backpack she was unzipping.

The guilt must have shown on my face, because Fiona looked back over her shoulder just as Darcy slid the infamous pink notebook out of Fiona's backpack.

"Hey!" Fiona yelled. "That's mine."

"Really?" Darcy said, smiling. "What is it?"

Fiona clumsily scrambled to her feet. It's hard to get out of a beanbag chair quickly, especially when you're wearing heels. "Give it to me! That's private!"

Darcy slid her finger underneath the cover. "Why, what's in it? Secrets? Gossip you spread about other kids?"

"What? No!" Fiona looked confused. "Give it back."

Fiona stretched out her hand to grab it, but it was just out of reach.

And too late. Darcy flipped the cover open for all of us to see what was inside.

I gasped.

Chapter 14

The pink notebook that Fiona kept with her all the time, that she scribbled in when she should have been paying attention to teachers, that Darcy was convinced contained all the secrets of the popular crowd, wasn't actually a notebook after all.

It was a sketchbook.

I stepped closer and watched as Darcy flipped through page after page of sketches. Shirts, skirts, and beautiful dresses. Some in color, some only pencil sketches.

"Did you draw these?" I asked.

Fiona snatched the book back and closed it. "Yes."

"Why didn't you want us to see that?" Darcy said. "I mean . . . it's good."

"You really think so?" Fiona asked, clutching the book to her chest.

Darcy shrugged. "Well, you should use fewer happy colors and more black, but yeah."

"Those are your own designs?" I asked.

Fiona nodded quickly. "Yeah. But don't tell anyone about it."

"Why not?" Darcy said. "There's great stuff in there."

"I don't know." Fiona stuffed the book back into her backpack. Then she turned to us. "I'd like to go to design school someday. Get into fashion. But I don't want anyone to know about it . . . in case I don't get in."

Hold up. Fiona Fanning — the most popular girl in our school — who had the looks, the clothes, the friends, the confidence . . . was afraid of failure.

I needed to sit down.

I slumped into a beanbag chair while Fiona and Darcy stayed standing.

"It's like one of those lifelong dreams," Fiona explained, twirling a strand of hair around her finger. "And I really want it to come true. But I'm scared that if I tell people, it will jinx it or something. Or that if I tell everyone and then I don't end up going to fashion school, it'll make the disappointment even worse."

Welcome to my nightmares, Fiona. Only substitute MIT for fashion school. Or Zane Munro liking me. Both cause equal anxiety.

"We won't tell anyone," I said, and Darcy nodded in agreement.

I had to admit, between Fiona needing our help and us seeing this other side of her, I was actually starting to like her a bit. We had as much in common as Jupiter and a pizza, but still. She was growing on me.

A pop song started coming from the backpacks on the bed.

"Oh, that's mine." Fiona unzipped the front pouch of her bag and pulled out a cell phone.

Seriously . . . was I the only girl in my grade without her own phone?

Fiona checked the screen to see who was calling. She giggled, then pressed a button to mute the music. "I'll call him back later," she explained.

"Who?" Darcy asked, taking a peek over Fiona's shoulder.

"Oh, it's just Slade," Fiona said. "He probably wanted to pick a day for our movie thing."

"Wait," Darcy said. "Slade Durkin? You're going on a date with Slade Durkin?"

Fiona slid her phone back into her bag. "We're going to meet at the movies sometime, that's all. It's no biggie."

Darcy looked so disgusted, it was as if Fiona told her she was planning to eat a bowl of live bugs for dinner. "What could you possibly see in him?" Darcy said.

Fiona examined her manicure. "Oh, I don't know. Maybe that he's popular. And the best in sports. And he's the tallest kid in our class and kind of cute."

"I think I'm going to throw up," Darcy said, clutching her stomach.

I tried to be a little less dramatic. "Fiona, he's kind of a . . . bully."

"What?" Fiona's eyes widened. "No, he's not. He's just a jokester."

I couldn't believe she didn't realize how much of a jerk Slade was. Yeah, he was never mean to *her*, but she had to have noticed how he treated the unpopular kids. I said, "You saw him hit Darcy in the face with a volleyball in gym."

"That was an accident," Fiona said.

"No, it wasn't." Darcy's voice was serious.

I nodded. "He told Darcy, 'That's for Hunter,' after he did it."

Fiona opened her mouth wide. "Well, um," she stuttered. "People are loyal to their friends. Darcy probably did something bad to Hunter and deserved it." After a quick look at Darcy's enraged face, she added, "No offense."

Though she needed no help from me, I felt the need to jump to Darcy's defense. "Darcy only did what she did because Hunter was torturing Zane."

"Yes," Darcy said teasingly. "Norah's true love."

"Darcy!" I snapped. I could feel my face getting all hot and red. I didn't need Fiona gossiping to everyone that I liked Zane. I turned to Fiona. "That's not true."

Thankfully, Fiona's phone started ringing again. I didn't care if it was Slade asking for her hand in marriage. Anything to get the conversation off Zane was fine with me.

"Hey, Mom," Fiona said. "I'm at Norah's." Pause. "Yes, the girl you met the other day." Pause. "I was just planning on walking —" Fiona rolled her eyes. "Fine!"

She stood and started repacking her things into her backpack. "Sorry to cut this short, but my mom's coming to pick me up."

"Remember to search your house for more clues about Bailey," Darcy said.

"I will," Fiona promised, heading out my bedroom door.

I could only hope she'd *forget* what she might have heard about me liking Zane Munro.

Chapter

15

The next morning, Darcy and I headed to our lockers together. I kept an eye out for Fiona, in case she might have any updates about what she'd found in her house.

The hallway was thick with kids, and everyone was walking so slowly. Like if we moved like snails, it would postpone the school day.

Darcy and I finally got to our lockers. I reached out to start the combination on my lock ... and froze.

"Um," I said, pointing. My locker door was half open.

"Did you forget to lock it when we left school yesterday?" Darcy asked.

I shook my head. My locker locks automatically when you close it, and I'd never once forgotten to close it all the way. I ran my finger down some scratches on the edge of the door. I'd never noticed those before.

"Norah," Darcy said worriedly, "it kind of looks like someone broke into your locker with a crowbar."

Dread churned in my stomach. Who would want to break into my locker? And why? I never left anything valuable in there. I'd brought most of my books home last night. Only two were left behind, and who'd want to steal those?

Or maybe . . . did Hunter or Slade leave something gross inside?

My hand trembled as I opened the door all the way. My two books were right as I'd left them in a neat pile. But on top of them was a folded piece of paper.

I pulled it out and looked at Darcy. Her eyes were wide. "Open it," she said.

I licked my lips nervously. My mouth felt so dry. I unfolded the paper. The words were typed, in a large font that took up the whole page.

NORAH & DARCY
BACK OFF THE CASE

The bell rang and the crowd all rushed inside their classrooms like a herd of animals heading for the stable. Darcy and I silently joined the stampede. A wave of nausea swept over me. Even Darcy seemed shaken. Her face was paler than usual and she was strangely quiet. We didn't speak until we slid into our desks at the start of first period.

"I can't believe that message," I said.

"It was more than a message," Darcy whispered back. "It was a threat."

"Who would've written that?" I asked.

Darcy slowly shook her head. "Someone who knows the truth and doesn't want us to find it."

Who could possibly know? I looked around the classroom. Was it someone in here? We had no evidence to tie to anyone. We couldn't compare handwriting samples because the note was typed.

The more I thought about the message, though, I felt angry rather than nervous. Who did this person think he or she was? Demanding that we back off. We were only trying to help someone. Someone who'd *asked* for our help. The nerve!

Mrs. Feldman walked to the front of the classroom and started writing on the board. Class was going to start any moment. I opened my textbook and clicked my pen.

"Well, we know one thing for sure," Darcy whispered, pulling out her notebook. "Someone doesn't want us to investigate anymore."

"But their plan is backfiring." I looked at Darcy with determination. "Because now I want to get to the bottom of this even more."

Chapter 16

In the hallway, on the way to second period, I found Fiona. She had her hair up and she fiddled with one of her long, dangly silver earrings as I approached.

"We need to meet again after school," I said in a low voice. "There have been . . . developments."

Fiona's face fell. "I have cheering practice after school."

Oh, man. We'd have to meet during the day, then. I thought for a moment. "We all have library fifth period, right?"

Fiona nodded with excitement. "Yeah. We can 'coincidentally' need to use the bathroom at the same time and have a short meeting in there."

I was surprised by Fiona's quick thinking. Maybe

she was sharper than I'd given her credit for. "See you there," I said and rushed off to my next class.

I filled Darcy in on our secret bathroom meeting plan over lunch. Fiona was acting her usual confident, giggly self over at the popular table. Now I understood that it was a good thing we didn't wave or acknowledge each other. Someone could be watching. Maybe the person who wrote that message.

I gave everyone second glances in fourth period — Hunter, Slade, Maya, even the teachers. I had to know. . . . Who wrote that message? And why did they so badly want us to stop investigating?

In library, Darcy and I sat at our usual round table. Fiona was at a different table a few bookcases away. She nodded at me. I cleared my throat. It was time.

Darcy stood first and quietly asked the librarian to be excused. A minute later, I asked. Mrs. Wixted, the librarian, didn't even raise an eyebrow. I wasn't known to waste precious study time, so she didn't figure I was lying. I gave Fiona one last glance as I left.

I'd only gotten halfway down the hall when Fiona trotted up next to me, her ponytail swinging from side to side.

"Any problem getting excused?" I whispered.

"No way," Fiona answered. "Mrs. Wixted would never think I'm leaving to hang with you two."

Insulting? Yes. But true? Yes.

I pushed open the heavy bathroom door and we silently entered. Darcy was bent over, looking under the stalls.

"The coast is clear," she said, straightening. She was chewing a giant wad of gum and blew a big purple bubble. It snapped and she pulled it back into her mouth.

I could use a little sugar, I thought. We weren't supposed to chew gum during class, but this was in the bathroom. I said, "Can I have a piece of gum?"

Unfortunately, Fiona asked at the exact same time.

Darcy pulled the package out of the pocket of her black hoodie. "I only have one piece left." She looked at both Fiona and me. "Okay, whoever gets closest. I'm thinking of a number between one and ten."

"Four!" Fiona screamed.

I hadn't even gotten a chance to *think* of a number yet.

"Wow, that was a fast response," Darcy said.

Fiona smiled. "My parents always say four is our

lucky number. And I was born on April fourth. Get it . . . four, four."

"Yeah, we get it," I said. "I'll choose seven."

Darcy tossed the last piece of gum to Fiona. "Lucky again. Sorry, Norah. My number was three."

Whatever. It was only gum. "Let's stop wasting time," I whispered. "We only have a few minutes in here until Mrs. Wixted starts to get suspicious."

Darcy opened her investigation notebook and jotted something down. What she could be writing about, I had no idea. Our little meeting hadn't even started yet. We walked past the two sinks and four stalls until we came to the far wall. We huddled around the window that was farthest from the door, in case of eavesdroppers.

"Did you search through your parents' stuff?" I asked Fiona.

She plopped the gum into her mouth and started chewing. "No, they never gave me the chance. They didn't leave me alone all night. Or even this morning."

Darcy and I sighed with disappointment.

"But I'm going to try again tonight," Fiona said. "Even if I have to wait until they go to bed."

"Good," I said, nodding.

Fiona snapped her gum. "So what's up with this emergency meeting?"

"I got a note in my locker," I explained. "It said: 'Norah and Darcy. Back off the case.'"

Fiona's eyebrows drew together. "That's kind of creepy."

"Really creepy," Darcy said. "But we're not scared. This person tells us to stop, but that only emboldens us further!"

Only Darcy would use a word like *emboldens*.

She held her fist out and I bumped it.

"Who do you think left the message?" Fiona asked.

Footsteps sounded from the hallway and we each held our breath. The footsteps stopped and then we heard the sound of a door opening.

But no one came in.

"The boys' room," I said. We all sighed in relief.

But, still, we had to hurry. If we stayed in the bathroom much longer, chances were someone would come in. Plus, Mrs. Wixted might start to suspect something was going on.

"Well," I said in a low voice. "Who else could know about the investigation? Who did you tell?"

"I didn't tell anyone!" Fiona swore, putting a hand to her chest. "You guys know how secretive this whole thing is to me. That's why I e-mailed you anonymously. Why I won't be seen with you guys during the school day. I don't want anyone to know. I haven't told a soul." Fiona turned to Darcy. "What about you?"

Darcy snickered. "My only friend is in this room. Who else *could* I tell?"

Fiona looked at me. "And you didn't tell anyone either?"

I started to shake my head no, but then Darcy said, "What about Zane?"

"What? Zane? No. He wouldn't." I stumbled over the words.

Fiona crossed her arms. "Zane Munro? What does he have to do with this? What did you tell him?"

"Nothing, nothing," I stammered. "He, uh, helped us get some information once. So he probably knows we're looking into something." Though I had slipped up and mentioned the word *case* to him when he gave me the Student Council papers. But he hadn't noticed it, right? I gulped and continued, "But he has no idea it's for you. And I don't know why he'd want us to back off. I mean, he helped us." I eyed

Darcy. "Come on, you know Zane didn't leave that message."

Darcy looked skeptical. "The thing is . . . he's the only other person at this school who knows we're up to something."

"Yeah, but he wouldn't try to scare us," I insisted.

"Do you know for sure?" Fiona asked.

Huh. I'd thought there was a chance Zane liked me . . . and then I saw him walking Maya home. Maybe I was wrong about this, too. "I guess it's possible," I admitted.

Darcy glanced at the clock. "We have to head back to the library. Next steps: Fiona, find clues at your house. Norah, find out what's up with Zane."

Chapter

17

For two weekends in a row, we had missed our Family Movie Night. So my parents insisted on having it Tuesday night because it was "important to spend time together." Even if we were sitting there not talking, shoving popcorn in our mouths.

My parents were cuddled together on one end of the couch, and Hubble and I were on the other. At one point during the movie, I glanced over at my parents. Mom's long blond hair was tied up in a ponytail and she wore jeans and a cute pink T-shirt. She looked younger and prettier than all the other moms in town.

Sometimes I wondered if Mom ever wished she'd

been the mother of one of those pretty girly-girls instead of someone like me. I don't like romance movies. I don't like to go shopping. I tend to wear comfortable clothes instead of worrying about trends and the latest fashions. And I don't wear makeup, though I let Mom do my face one time, mostly to make her happy. I think she knew I didn't enjoy it, though, because she never asked again.

Sometimes I wished I could magically be interested in the things Mom likes. Because I was worried that she was disappointed that she'd had a daughter like me. I was worried that she wished she had a daughter like Fiona.

On Wednesday, I was on my way to the cafeteria for lunch when I realized I'd left one of my notebooks behind in the library. I groaned and doubled back. The room was empty. Even Mrs. Wixted was out. Probably having lunch in the teachers' lounge.

I had been doing work at a small table around the corner behind the science fiction books. I rounded the corner, ready to grab my notebook and hurry to the cafeteria. But instead I found that I wasn't alone.

Startled, my hand went to my heart. It was pounding like a sledgehammer. "I didn't know anyone else was in here," I said.

Maya looked so small seated at the table with a sandwich in her hand. "Sorry," she squeaked.

My heartbeat started to return to normal. "What are you doing in here?"

"Eating lunch," Maya said.

"Yeah, but why are you eating in here all alone?"

So softly that I could barely hear her, Maya said, "I've been eating here a lot lately."

"Oh," I said. Mainly because I couldn't think of anything else to say. She looked down again at her sandwich. The crusts were cut off. She must have not been a fan of crusts. Neither was I.

I pulled out the chair opposite her and sat down. "If you ever want to eat in the cafeteria, you can sit with Darcy and me."

She nodded but didn't look up. "Yeah, maybe sometime."

I thought about my assignment for our investigation. I didn't have the guts to ask Zane what was going on with him. But maybe I could find out an easier way. . . .

"So, um, what's going on with you and Zane Munro?" I asked.

Maya's head snapped up and her eyes widened. "Nothing! Nothing at all!"

I'd never heard her speak so loudly. That wasn't the reaction I was expecting. She seemed . . . nervous. I said, "I was just wondering —"

Maya interrupted me. "I have to go." She picked up the remains of her lunch and stood to leave.

I held up a hand. "Wait. Why are you so nervous?"

Maya chewed her lip for a second. "I can't talk about it," she said.

"Talk about *what*?"

"Zane's secret." As soon as Maya said the words, she squealed in horror, dropped her lunch, clasped both hands over her mouth, and ran away.

AFTER school, Darcy, Fiona, and I walked home together. I so desperately wanted to tell Darcy about Maya's freak-out in the library. But I worried that she'd just assume Zane's secret was about the note in my locker. And I still didn't think he'd do something like that.

We went to Darcy's house this time. As we grabbed some snacks from the kitchen, Fiona asked, "Where's your mom?"

"Work," Darcy said, shoving a pretzel the size of my face into her mouth.

"Does she work every day?" Fiona asked.

Darcy nodded. She couldn't really speak. Due to the giant pretzel.

"You have the house to yourself every afternoon?" Fiona sighed. "Oh, man, I'm so jealous of you guys."

Darcy and I shared a skeptical look. Fiona Fanning was jealous of *us*?

"The whole house to yourself every afternoon," Fiona said dreamily. "Your mom is probably the type to let you do whatever you want, too, isn't she?"

Darcy shrugged a yes. She was still eating that pretzel.

Fiona turned to me. "And your mom is so pretty and cool. She was a cheerleader at our school, did you know that? And your dad was this big jock. There are trophies with his name on them in the glass case in the school hallway. You must be so proud."

"Yeah, I guess." I'd never really thought of Mom and Dad as parents other kids would envy me for. They were just, you know, my parents.

Darcy pointed upstairs to tell us we should go to her room. Thankfully, by the time we got up there, she could talk again. I slid into the bacon chair.

Darcy's closet was open and Fiona peeked inside.

"Your whole wardrobe is black and purple," she said, aghast.

"Yeah, so?" Darcy said, leaning back in a chair.

"Well, don't you own anything that doesn't look like it's for a Halloween theme day?"

"I have my style. You have yours." Darcy chomped on another pretzel. "So are you going out with that disgusting Slade this weekend?"

Fiona hopped onto Darcy's bed and crossed her legs. "Nah, I pushed him off until next weekend. I have too much to do right now with cheering, homework, an absolutely crucial trip to the mall, and of course this investigation. Plus, he wants to double, so I have to organize that."

"Double-date? With who?" Darcy asked.

"One of my cheerleader friends," Fiona said casually.

"Yeah, but which friend of his?" Darcy asked again.

"Hunter," she admitted.

"Oh, double puke!" Darcy exclaimed.

"Can we focus here, girls?" I said.

Darcy reached into the bag for another giant pretzel, and I grabbed it out of her hand. "Seriously. Let's go over anything we've learned since our last meeting."

I wasn't quite ready to tell them about Zane, so I said to Fiona, "Did you find any other clues in your house?"

Her shoulders sagged. "No. And they've started keeping the den locked, which is strange."

"They've never locked it before?" Darcy asked.

"Nope. And I tried eavesdropping last night when they were talking in there, but all I heard was something about someone who's moving."

They could have been talking about *anyone*. "That doesn't help much," I said.

Darcy's laptop made a pinging sound and she picked it up off the floor and slid it onto her lap.

"What's that?" Fiona asked.

"It's a computer," Darcy said.

Fiona rolled her eyes.

Darcy laughed. "It's my tone for new e-mail."

She keyed in her password. As she read the e-mail, her face changed. I knew immediately this wasn't good.

"What?" I asked.

Darcy looked up at me, then at Fiona. "I think we just heard from whoever left the note."

Chapter 18

"What does it say?" Fiona and I asked at the same time.

Darcy cleared her throat. Gripping the laptop tightly, she read the e-mail out loud. "'Darcy and Norah: Stop. You are putting Fiona's life . . . in danger.'"

The little blond hairs on my arms stood up as a chill went through my whole body.

Fiona said anxiously, "Can I see that?"

Darcy walked the laptop over to the bed, where Fiona was sitting, and placed it on her lap. Darcy and I sat on either side of her and read the message again and again. The e-mail address was unfamiliar — just a random string of numbers. Whoever was sending us these messages meant business.

"How could we be putting her life in danger?" I wondered out loud.

"Maybe we are," Darcy said. "Or maybe we aren't."

"What do you mean?" Fiona asked with a quiver in her voice.

"Whoever this person is, he or she realized that the note didn't stop us from investigating. So they're trying something different. Instead of ordering us to back off, they're giving us this life-or-death warning. Thinking maybe that will work."

I wrung my hands together nervously. "But what if they're telling the truth? What if we really *are* putting her in danger?" *And ourselves, too,* I thought.

Darcy cracked her knuckles. "Okay, give me back the computer. It's time for Senora Hacker to get to work."

Fiona handed the laptop over. "What are you going to do?"

"Give me five minutes," Darcy answered. "I'm going to find out who this person is."

"How?" I said.

"After all the anonymous e-mails we got from our client" — she motioned at Fiona — "I decided to research e-mail-tracing software programs. I convinced my mom to get me one." She grinned and said conspiratorially, "I told her it was an educational game."

I rolled my eyes at Darcy's behavior but was secretly glad she'd done it.

Darcy grinned at me. "Anyway, it's complicated and involves Internet Protocol addresses and stuff that would bore you as much as your chattering on about astronomy bores me."

"Point taken," I said. "Do your thing." Sometimes it was best to just let Darcy work.

Fiona and I had a staring contest with the floor, silently sitting, waiting for news. My pulse was racing. When five minutes turned to ten, I started to wonder. Darcy was a computer genius. When she said something was going to take her five minutes, that meant three. Something was up.

Darcy's narrowed eyes stared at the screen as she pounded the keyboard and grunted and groaned. If looks could kill, that laptop would've been on fire. Finally, after another few minutes, Darcy slammed it closed.

"What's up?" I said, almost too scared to ask.

She let out a long exhale. "Well, I don't think it's anyone from our school."

"Really?" Fiona's voice bubbled with excitement. "Your computer program told you that?"

"Tone it down, Happy Pants," Darcy said. "This is *bad* news."

"Why?" I asked.

"Some kid at school couldn't do what this person did." Darcy paused. "The e-mail is encrypted."

"What's that?" Fiona asked, much less excited now.

"It means that the person who sent the e-mail was technologically savvy enough to hide the e-mail's origins. I can't find out for sure where it came from. But that tells us one thing."

I gulped. "What?"

Darcy shifted her gaze out the window. "That we're dealing with something much bigger than we imagined."

"Like . . . dangerous people?" Fiona said in a small voice.

"Maybe," Darcy said.

I put my hand on Fiona's shoulder. "Do you want to stop the investigation?"

She looked down at her hands and thought for a long moment. Then she straightened her posture and said, "No. I want to keep going until I find out the truth."

I was glad she said that, because I felt the same way. We had come so far and were in so deep. We couldn't quit now. I looked at Darcy and nodded slightly.

Darcy said, "Okay, then, Fiona. If you're still in, we're still in."

Fiona forced a nervous smile. "Thanks, guys. So, what now?"

"I think it's time to talk to your parents," I suggested.

Fiona shook her head quickly. "My parents are so overprotective. If they find out someone is kind of threatening me, they will freak out and never let me out of the house again!"

"But what if they know something?" I said. "They might be able to steer us toward who's doing this. They had Bailey's birth certificate, after all."

"This is bigger than my parents," Fiona said. "This is like . . . like . . . a conspiracy! My parents wouldn't know anything about crypticized e-mails —"

"Encrypted," Darcy corrected.

"Yeah, whatever," Fiona continued. "They wouldn't know anything. My mom can barely coordinate tops with skirts."

I got up and started pacing the room. Fiona was insistent on not telling her parents. But I couldn't think of any other next step to take. This is when I usually counted on Darcy to come up with something brilliant, but she was staring into space. Fiona nervously twirled a strand of hair around her finger.

After a few minutes of silence, Darcy stood and faced Fiona. "Okay. Your parents might hold a clue to this mystery, but I understand if you don't want to ask them. That just means there's only one thing for us to do."

Fiona pulled her hand from her hair. "What?"

Darcy smiled mischievously. "We're going to spy on your parents."

Chapter 19

Friday night, I went to the movies with a boy, and then we went to the most popular girl in school's birthday party!

Just kidding. I went to Darcy's house and we got pizza. But it was still probably the most exciting Friday night I'd ever had. Because I was getting ready to go undercover.

We were sitting at her dining room table with a pepperoni pizza, a laptop, and a checklist. Darcy's mom was watching a movie in the other room. When she'd asked us if we wanted to join her, Darcy said, "No thanks, Mom. We have a secret stakeout mission tomorrow and we have to plan."

"Okay, honey," her mom called over her shoulder.

I raised my eyebrows. I didn't know if she thought Darcy was joking or if she was just too tired to deal with it. Either way, it was time to get to work.

Darcy scanned the list. "Okay, I think we have all the equipment we need. Don't forget your part."

I nodded. "I know where to bring my telescope in the morning." I took a bite of the pizza slice, holding it tightly so the cheese wouldn't slide off and land on my chin. "Does Fiona know everything she has to do?"

Darcy nodded, but looked worried. "I went over everything twice. Hopefully, she remembers."

I wiped my hands with a napkin and slid her laptop over to me. "Mind if I go online? I want to do a little research on Fiona and Bailey's place of birth."

"Sure thing. I've been working on something in my clue book anyway."

I typed *Garretson, South Dakota*, into the search engine and clicked on the first listing. It was an online encyclopedia that would give me some general information about the place. I took a few minutes to read through everything.

"Find anything interesting?" Darcy asked, tapping a pencil on her head.

"Well, it's home to Devil's Gulch."

Darcy looked up. "Cool name! What's that?"

"A place where that outlaw from the 1800s, Jesse James, nearly got captured. But he escaped by riding a horse over a twenty-foot gorge."

"Whoa." Darcy gave an impressed nod. "Anything more recent?"

"Yeah, looks like Jesse James wasn't the only outlaw to hide in Garretson. Some guy who'd wronged the mob in the New York City was hiding out there, thinking they'd never find him in South Dakota."

"Let me guess, he thought wrong."

"Yeah, the mob boss caught up with him and killed him. Unfortunately there was a witness." I squinted at the screen. "Some guy named Neil."

Darcy let out a low whistle. "I bet things didn't turn out well for him. They never do."

Totally. I remembered an episode of *Crime Scene: New York* that Darcy made me watch that had a similar story line.

But I had to focus back on Bailey and Fiona's place of birth. I scanned the rest of the information. "Wow," I said. "I thought Danville was small. Garretson has less than twelve hundred people."

Darcy shrugged. "Mr. Fanning probably moved the family here for a job."

"Yeah." I sighed. "But we're still no closer to figuring out where Bailey went." I pointed at her notebook. "What are you working on there?"

"This could just be a coincidence, but I figured out something kind of cool. Remember how Fiona said four is the family's lucky number?"

"Yeah . . ." I remembered when Darcy jotted something down in the investigation notebook that day in the bathroom. It must have been that fact about the number four.

"Well, if you add four to each letter of the alphabet, the initials *BAB* become *FEF*."

I pictured the alphabet in my mind. Darcy was right. If you're at *B* and then you move down four letters, you get *F*. If you're at *A* and move down four letters, you get *E*. I gasped. "So Bailey Ann Banks plus four is Fiona Erin Fanning."

"Yeah!" Darcy said, but then frowned. "I don't know if it means anything, though. It could just be a coincidence."

Darcy's find *was* cool. And it might mean nothing. But Mrs. Fanning loved puzzles. It would make sense that she'd name her children using some kind of code. That didn't get us any closer to finding Bailey, though.

We'd have to make a breakthrough tomorrow. If our plan didn't work . . . we might never find out the truth.

Chapter 20

I felt like a real undercover detective. We had our spy gadgets, we had a plan, and now all we had to do was put it into action.

But first . . . cheerleading.

I'd never gone to a sports game of any kind at Danville Middle School. But sometimes, in undercover work, you have to pretend to be something you're not. Like someone who has school spirit. So on Saturday, Darcy and I showed up at the school fields, ready to cheer on our team.

"What sport does Fiona do cartwheels for again?" Darcy asked as we walked behind the school.

"Football," I said. Behind our school were two large

fields surrounded by a track for running. It looked like both fields were being used. Soccer in the front field, football in the back. I pointed at the far field, where a bunch of girls on the sidelines were pumping their pom-poms in the air. "She's down there."

Darcy heaved a sigh. "Okay, let's go pretend we care if our school wins or not."

I bumped her with my elbow. "It won't be that bad. Look at the scoreboard. We timed it perfectly."

As part of the plan, we needed to meet Fiona here. But of course we didn't want to sit through an entire game. So I'd found out the start time, Googled how long a middle school football game lasts on average, and figured out approximately what time we'd have to get there for only five minutes to be left in the game. The scoreboard showed seven minutes left. Very close! If there weren't a bunch of parents and kids watching from the bleachers, I would've reached over and patted myself on the back.

The soccer game was ending as we passed by. Dozens of sweaty boys in uniform ran off the field as coaches and parents high-fived them. The team in white jerseys seemed to be happier, so they must have won. Whether they were our team or the other town, I didn't know, and I wasn't planning on getting close enough to any of the sweaty boys to find out.

Until I heard my name.

"Hey, Norah!"

I stopped and started looking around, but Darcy must have figured it out before I did, because she gave me a sneaky smile and whispered, "I'll meet you over there."

I felt a tap on my shoulder and turned to face Zane. His hair was all wet and crazy and he had a dirt streak on one cheek. But he was still cute.

He wore one of the white jerseys, with the telltale word *Danville* written above the number on his chest.

"Congrats on the win!" I said.

He took a giant gulp from his water bottle, then said, panting, "Thanks. It was a tough game. I'm glad we were able to pull out a win with that final goal. Did you see it?"

My thoughts raced. *Should I lie and say I did? But then what if he asks me a question about it and I can't answer and I look stupid? Oh, man, why do I always get tongue-tied around him? I'm smart. I had the vocabulary of a fifth grader by kindergarten, but I cannot form a single sentence right now!*

Since my voice box was in panic mode, I just did this jerky body movement that was half shrug and half shake of the head.

"So Maya told me she saw you in the library the other day," Zane said.

It seemed like those two shared all their secrets.

"She said you invited her to sit with you and Darcy at lunch," he continued. "That was nice. I've offered that before, too, but she doesn't want to sit with a bunch of guys."

Ugh. Why didn't they just get a romantic table for two in the corner? That ugly green monster — jealousy — was starting to rise up in me and I wasn't proud of it. I told myself it wasn't Maya's fault Zane liked her instead of me.

"I just wanted her to know she didn't have to eat alone," I said.

Zane smiled. "That's really cool of you. Maya lives on my street, you know."

Here we go. Here's where he was going to tell me their whole love story. I was going to throw up on the soccer field.

Zane continued, "That jerk Hunter Fisk lives on the street next to ours. He's been giving her a hard time. Name-calling and stuff while she walked home from school all alone. So I've been walking her home for the last week or so. It seems to have helped. Hunter's moved on to bullying someone else for the time being."

Wait . . . what? Zane was only walking Maya home to protect her? Did this mean . . . ?

I blurted out, "So you're not boyfriend and girlfriend?"

Zane's face turned as red as Mars. (Known as the red planet. Though it's really more rust-colored, if you ask me.) He scratched at the back of his neck. His eyes stared at the ground. "No. I, uh, don't have a girlfriend."

Then he looked up. Right into my eyes.

I felt my face getting hot. I imagined it as a big giant burning surface, like the sun, with solar flares shooting out of my pores as each second of silence dragged on. My mind yelled at my mouth. *Say something, stupid!*

Zane looked back down. "Okay, well, I should go. My parents are here somewhere."

And then, before I could say anything, he'd wandered away to the bleachers.

And I stood there wondering: If nothing was going on between him and Maya . . . then what was Zane's big secret?

Chapter 21

By the time I got over to the football sidelines, the game had ended. Darcy and Fiona looked so strange standing together. Darcy wore jeans, her black Converse sneakers, and a black T-shirt with white lettering that read WHY BE NORMAL? Fiona, meanwhile, had her hair up in a pink ribbon and wore her cheerleading uniform. And they were chatting. *If these two could act friendly,* I thought, *maybe there's hope for peace between all nations. Cats and dogs. Vampires and werewolves.*

"It's about time you finished talking to Zane," Darcy told me, and made an awkward kissing face.

"You look like a fish drowning in air," I said. "Where are we with the plan?"

"The game just ended," Fiona said. "My parents are sitting over there. Let's do this."

Mr. and Mrs. Fanning sat prim and proper in the front row of the bleachers. Fiona's little sister, Mia, sat between them, playing a handheld video game. Confused looks colored her parents' faces as the three of us approached.

Fiona lovingly ruffled Mia's hair, then got down to business, putting on an Academy Award–worthy performance. "Oh my God, Mom! I totally, totally, totally forgot that, like, I have to work on a class project today with Norah and Darcy. And it's, like, totally due Monday. So we have to, like, totally go do it now at Norah's house."

Mrs. Fanning frowned. "I don't remember you saying you had a project."

"Well, duh," Fiona said. "I forgot!"

"Though it's a good project," Darcy said with a sparkle in her eye. "It's very . . . mysterious."

Mrs. Fanning opened her mouth to say something else, but Fiona said, "So I'll see you later back at the house!"

Mia shouted, "'Bye, Fiona," but never looked up from her game.

With a quick wave, Fiona turned and linked arms with Darcy and me, and we walked down the track like Dorothy, Scarecrow, and Tin Man down the yellow brick road.

When we got to the back wall of the school near the bike rack, we hid around a corner. Darcy poked her head out and peered into the parking lot.

"Anything?" Fiona asked.

"Not yet . . . okay, yeah. There they are, walking to their car."

I leaned over Darcy's kneeling body and took a peek for myself. Fiona's parents stopped briefly outside their black car. Mrs. Fanning's arms flailed in the air like an angry bird. Was she upset that Fiona forgot about a project? Or mad that she was hanging out with us? Or something more?

Then they got in the car and drove away.

"We're clear," I said.

"Good." Darcy went over to the bike rack and unlocked two bikes. She pushed one to Fiona.

"What's this?" Fiona looked at the bike in disgust. It was a beat-up, black, boys' bike that had definitely seen better days. I recognized it as Darcy's old bike from before she'd gotten her new one. Which was also black. And a boys' one.

"Walking will take too long," Darcy said. "We have to bike there or we'll miss a big chunk of conversation."

Fiona crossed her arms and refused to take it. "I won't be caught dead on that bike."

Darcy groaned. "That can be arranged. . . ."

"Here," I said, pulling my red bike out of the rack. "You take mine. I'll ride Darcy's old bike. Let's just get going."

Ten minutes later, we were in the woods behind Fiona's house. We biked there as fast as we could and entered the forest a few houses down by cutting through the yard of an empty house that was for sale. Our stuff was all ready for us, right where we'd left it that morning.

The woods were quiet and kind of creepy, even though it was a bright sunny day. But the adrenaline rush of excitement was overwhelming any nervous feelings I had. I felt like a real private investigator on a big, dangerous mission. This was so much cooler than how I usually spent my Saturday afternoons.

The woods faced the back of Fiona's house. My telescope was aimed at one of the house's many windows. I looked through the scope and adjusted the focus. When we had decided to spy on Fiona's parents, we knew we needed some gear. Fiona's innocent comment about my telescope had given me the idea to bring it out here. Sure, I'd only pointed it at the stars before, but that didn't mean it *couldn't* be used for spying on people.

I had a clear view of the house. Mia ran upstairs, probably to play. Mr. and Mrs. Fanning were in the kitchen, right where we needed them to be. I tried to read their lips, but they kept moving around the room too much. It wasn't too hard to read their emotions, though. Red faces, hands flying through the air, mouths moving quickly. They were completely freaking out.

"They're in the kitchen," I said. "Take it off mute! Now!"

Darcy lifted her cell phone from the large rock we'd left it on, turned on the speakerphone, and turned up the volume. Immediately, Mr. and Mrs. Fanning's voices filled the air.

Darcy had come up with this idea. She'd told

Fiona to make sure her phone was fully charged. Then, before she left for the game, she was to call Darcy's phone. Darcy would answer. But they wouldn't talk. They wouldn't hang up, either. They'd leave the line open.

Then Fiona would plant her cell phone somewhere in her kitchen. Not under too much stuff (so it could pick up conversation), but not in plain sight (so it wouldn't be found). Then we'd be able to sit out here and listen on Darcy's phone. It worked just like how cops bugged bad guys' houses. Pure genius.

"It might be time to do it again," Mrs. Fanning said.

I watched through the telescope as their voices came across the cell phone. Mrs. Fanning looked less angry now and more depressed.

Mr. Fanning let out a loud sigh. "But how will we get new —" The last word was muffled.

"New what?" Fiona whispered.

Darcy shrugged. I looked back through the scope.

Mrs. Fanning tapped her fingernails on the kitchen counter. "We have to get in touch with our contact at the program."

Mr. Fanning rubbed his hands down his face. "I really wish it hadn't come to this."

"Me, too, Neil," Mrs. Fanning agreed. "But it's gone too far."

Mr. Fanning put an arm around his wife and gently led her out of the kitchen. I tried to follow them with my scope, but they went into his office, which faced the side of the house.

"We're out of range of the phone," I said, and lifted my eyes from the scope. My thoughts were racing.

Darcy groaned. "What are we going to do now? Hope they go back to the kitchen?"

I took a deep breath. Everything we'd learned over the past few days had been floating around in my head like mismatched puzzle pieces. But one final word that Mrs. Fanning had spoken just made all the pieces click together.

"We don't need them to," I said. "I figured out what's going on." I turned to Fiona. "I know where Bailey is."

Chapter 22

Fiona stood in the woods behind her house, looking out of place in her cheerleading uniform. Her ponytail trembled as she said, "You know where my twin is?"

"There was never any twin," I said. "Fiona . . . *you're* Bailey Banks."

Darcy put the cell phone down and sat on the big rock, eyes wide. "Norah, you're going to have to explain this theory."

I nodded, excited by how sure I was. I couldn't believe how much sense it all made, now that I thought about it. "Fiona was born Bailey Banks," I said, "but then — at some point — her parents changed her name to Fiona Fanning."

"But what about the baby pictures?" Fiona asked.

"One is you," I said. "But the other is probably just your sister, Mia."

Darcy said, "Mia *is* like a little Mini-You."

Fiona brought her hand up to her cheek. "I remember when Mia was born, Mom said she looked exactly like I had. I hadn't even considered that the pictures could be of Mia and me." She brought her hand down as confusion returned to her face. "But why would they change my name?"

I tried to think of how to put all my thoughts in some kind of order. I decided to just lay out the evidence — piece by piece. "Fiona, your house is — no offense — very ordinary. It's an average house. It just blends in. Same with your parents' car. It looks like every other car. Nothing about your parents stands out."

"So?" Darcy said. "Lots of people are like that."

"But it's almost like they're going out of their way to blend in. Plus, there's more." I took a deep breath and continued. "Your mom loves solving puzzles. So much so that, when she changed Bailey's name, she even used a code."

Darcy took a minute to explain the shifted-alphabet code to Fiona. How the initials BAB became FEF.

"And your dad," I said, "is really good with computers. He works on them all day long. . . ."

I glanced at Darcy, who gave herself a facepalm. "I can't believe I didn't think of that before!" she said. "He would totally know how to encrypt an e-mail."

I went on. "Last night, Darcy and I did some research on the place Bailey was born — Garretson, South Dakota. It's a small town where nothing much really happens. Their biggest story of the century was about a criminal who went there to hide from the mob. But the mob found him and killed him . . . right in front of a witness."

Fiona's face scrunched up. "I still don't get it. What does that have to do with my family?"

"The newspaper article didn't print the witness's last name, to protect him, but his first name was Neil."

Fiona paled. "I thought . . . I just heard . . ." She stammered as she pointed to the cell phone on the rock. "I thought I heard my mom just call my father Neil, but his name is Roger. I figured I heard it wrong since the reception is kind of bad."

When Mrs. Fanning had first said it, for a split second I'd thought I'd misheard it, too. But then the name sounded familiar. I remembered the witness in the article I'd read last night and everything clicked together.

"No," I said. "You heard it right. Your mom got so emotional that she slipped and called him his real name. I think your father is Neil Banks."

Darcy gasped. "Add four like the code and NB becomes RF . . . Roger Fanning."

"So my dad witnessed a murder?" Fiona's voice shook.

"And your whole family had to change their names and go into hiding," I said.

Darcy snapped her fingers. "Mrs. Fanning just said they need to talk to their contact at the program. They must be in the Witness Protection Program." She started pacing frantically. "It all makes sense now. Everything makes sense."

"Will someone please explain it to *me*?" Fiona yelled.

I said, "The Witness Protection Program helps people move away and sets them up with new identities so the bad guys won't . . . you know . . . get them."

This also explained why Fiona's parents were so ridiculously overprotective.

Darcy added breathlessly, "And the government has enough power to make an old identity disappear, too. That's why Bailey seemed to not exist anywhere."

At that moment, someone started slowly clapping. We'd all been so enthralled in my explanation that we hadn't been watching the house. We hadn't seen two people approach the woods. And now they were standing behind us.

Fiona's parents.

Mr. Fanning, in jeans and a misbuttoned shirt, looked outright downtrodden. His face sagged. Dark bags circled his eyes. Mrs. Fanning wore a trench coat over her outfit. She looked just plain angry.

Shocked, Fiona said, "How did you know we were out here?"

"We went into the office to look up the GPS on your phone to check on where you were," Mr. Fanning started.

"You monitor my location?" Fiona asked, open-mouthed. "Often?"

"Of course." Mrs. Fanning shrugged. "Why else would we have gotten you a cell phone? We need to know where you are at all times. And this time, you lied. You were not at Norah's house. In fact, your cell phone was in the kitchen."

She pulled Fiona's cell out of her pocket and showed us. It was still on. They'd found the phone through their GPS tracking, picked it up, and listened to *us*.

They'd heard every word we'd said.

I looked from Fiona to her parents and back again as they stared each other down. It was almost like a contest to see who would break down and speak first.

Fiona said, "Is it true?"

Mrs. Fanning stepped closer to her daughter and said in a soft voice. "Yes. You are Bailey Banks. Mia has always been Mia because she was born after we had to flee. But your father, Roger Fanning, is Neil Banks. And I, Maura Fanning, am Irene Banks. We lived in Garretson, South Dakota."

"Until the murder," Fiona said.

Mr. Fanning stepped forward. "I had to testify against one of the biggest criminal bosses in the country. It wasn't safe for us to stay there. The government helped us move here to Danville. Your mother picked our new names, the government took care of all the identity switching."

"Why didn't you tell me?" The hurt in Fiona's voice was clear and I understood why. I couldn't imagine my parents keeping a secret like this from me.

Mrs. Fanning looked down at the ground. "You were just a baby when we had to leave. We knew you'd remember nothing of our past life. And we thought it was best not to tell you. We didn't want to you be scared."

"You put the threat in my locker," I asked. "And e-mailed us to stop investigating."

"Yes," Mr. Fanning said. "I didn't want the truth to come out. It could put all our lives in danger."

"How did you even know I'd contacted Norah and Darcy for help?" Fiona asked.

Mr. Fanning explained with an embarrassed grin, "We monitor your e-mail."

Fiona's face turned red with rage. "You follow my whereabouts on my cell phone! You read all my e-mails!"

"It's only to protect you, honey." Mrs. Fanning reached out her arms, but Fiona backed away, still angry.

Mrs. Fanning crossed her arms and frowned. "Well, we've loved our new life here in Danville with you and your sister. But now," she turned to Darcy and me, "you nosy girls have gone and ruined the life we've built for ourselves here."

Her eyes turned stern and determined. She straightened and reached into the side pocket of her coat. "I'm sorry, Fiona," she said, though her eyes were glued to Darcy and me. "I'm afraid there's only one thing we can do now."

Chapter

23

"What are you going to do to them?" Fiona screeched.

Darcy looked skeptical, but my stomach was spinning like Mom's KitchenAid mixer on its highest setting.

Mrs. Fanning pulled her hand out of her jacket pocket and in it was . . . a folded-up map. "Do to who?"

"Norah and Darcy, to keep them quiet," Fiona said softly.

Mrs. Fanning rolled her eyes. "Nothing. However, your friends are going to leave now and we're going to open this map and pick a new place to live."

"We have to move?" Fiona whined.

"Yes," Mr. Fanning said. "And choose new names again, of course."

Fiona burst into tears. "But I don't want to! I like my life here. I'm popular. What if we move to a new town and I become a friendless loser?"

Oh, the horror, I thought. But I did feel sorry for her. I couldn't imagine being uprooted from my life. Having to leave the only town I'd ever known. My best friend. Other people (coughZanecough).

Mr. Fanning looked like *he* was going to cry at the sight of his daughter breaking down. But Mrs. Fanning only shook her head sadly. "Honey, we tried to protect you," she said softly. "We tried to keep you out of harm's way. But you involved these girls and they figured everything out. It's your fault, Fiona."

This only made Fiona cry harder.

"Actually," Darcy said, stepping in between Fiona and her mother, "it's *your* fault. Have you ever heard of honesty?"

Mrs. Fanning said simply, "We had to leave that behind in South Dakota."

"Well, then, how about trust?" I said. I moved to one side of Fiona and grabbed her arm. Darcy held her other arm.

Darcy said, "If you had trusted your daughter and she'd known the truth, she wouldn't have come to us for help. And we'd have never found out about your past. It's your distrust that caused all of this."

"Please, Mom." Tears streamed down Fiona's cheeks. "This is my life. I don't want to become someone else. I'll never tell anyone our family secret, and neither will Norah and Darcy."

Mrs. Fanning frowned. "I can't just take their word for it, honey."

Mr. Fanning coughed into his hand and stepped closer to his wife. "Maybe these girls are right. Maybe we should give trust a try."

Mrs. Fanning rubbed her face with her hands. After a few moments of considering us with narrowed eyes, she said, "I suppose we *could* always keep one suitcase each packed, just in case they told."

I felt a burst of hope. "We wouldn't tell," I said firmly, and Darcy nodded, just as strongly.

Mrs. Fanning studied us closely. "So you girls promise to keep our old identity a secret?"

Darcy said, "Heck yeah!" She loved being in on secrets, and this was about the biggest one of our lives.

Relief washed over me as I said, "I promise, too." I

would've felt horrible if our investigation had forced Fiona to give up her life, move away, and change her name.

"Thank you, guys," Fiona said to us, still looking tearful but no longer as distraught. To my surprise, she reached over and gave me, and then Darcy, a quick hug. Then she turned around, and her parents wrapped her in a giant, three-person hug.

Darcy and I looked at each other, knowing we should give the Fannings — or the Bankses — their time alone. We collected our spy gear and headed back to my house. The investigation was over. Bailey Ann Banks was where she belonged.

On Sunday, Darcy and I baked cupcakes in her kitchen. Not regular cupcakes. Celebration cupcakes. I expected them to taste even sweeter.

We'd frosted them — yellow for me and chocolate for Darcy. While we stood waiting for them to cool (note: staring at cupcakes does not make them cool any faster), I thought about the case. It was funny . . . at the beginning I hadn't even really wanted to get involved. But now I was so glad I had. We'd helped

Fiona learn the truth about herself and her family. Darcy got some excitement in her life, which she always loves. And me? I felt proud.

Less than three weeks ago, I was terrified to stand in front of class and give a presentation on a fake detective agency. And now? I'd hunted down clues, done a stakeout, and unmasked fake identities. Not too shabby for a goody-goody.

The only downside? I was kind of sad that everything was over. I had gotten to like all that intrigue. Maybe I'd start watching *Crime Scene: New York* every week with Darcy.

"The cupcakes should be cool enough by now," Darcy said.

We reached in and pulled a cupcake each out of the pan. I felt like we should mark the moment somehow. I held my cupcake out. "To us figuring out a mystery."

Darcy smiled and bumped my cupcake with hers. "To Partners in Crime and our first case."

I had already taken a bite when that word hit my brain. "First?" I said.

"You really shouldn't talk with your mouth full," Darcy teased.

I swallowed. "What do you mean . . . first?"

Darcy tilted her head side to side with a sneaky smile on her face. "I didn't take the website down yet. If we want to . . . we can leave it up."

"And accept more cases? How would we even get the word out? It's not like we can advertise that we're a real detective agency. We're seventh graders!" These questions came pouring out of my mouth because that's me — logical. But inside, I was thrilled by the idea of working on another case.

"We can figure all that out as we go," Darcy said and shoved half a cupcake into her mouth.

And, for now, that was good enough for me.

Chapter

24

I had assumed Fiona was an airhead who only cared about clothes and makeup. But I was wrong. Well, she does care about clothes and makeup. A lot. But those aren't the only things she cares about. She loves her little sister. She values the truth. And . . . as Darcy and I found out at school Monday morning, she can be a good friend.

Darcy and I were standing at our lockers, trying to act normal after the Craziest Weekend Ever. Fiona strutted up to us, gliding gloss onto her lips as she walked. She stopped at our lockers — for the first time.

"Want to try?" she said, holding out the lip gloss. "It's Very Berry flavor."

"Um, no thanks," Darcy said.

"How are you?" I asked softly.

"Great!" And from her beaming smile, I knew she meant it. "Things have really changed with my parents. We had some good talks this weekend. They told me stories about 'everything that happened,' if you know what I mean. I always thought of them as lame dorks. Buth they're actually very brave and cool." She shrugged and dropped her voice to a whisper. "Even if no one can know about it."

"That's great," I said. "We're really happy for you."

Well, I knew I was happy. I assumed it was the same with Darcy, but she wasn't a "let's talk about our emotions" kind of gal.

"One more thing," Fiona said. "I texted Slade and told him the double date wasn't going to happen. Ever. He texted back asking why and I replied . . ." She smiled. "Well, let me just show you."

She slipped her phone out of her bag, scrolled down to find the text, and held it up for us to see.

That's for Darcy and Norah.

Darcy's eyes widened. "No. Way."
Fiona giggled. "Yes, I did."

"That's awesome!" I said.

"So . . ." Fiona looked down at her heeled boots, almost shyly. "I have a question. If your detective agency gets another case . . . could I maybe help you guys again?"

A few weeks ago, the idea of me spending time with Fiona Fanning would have been laughable. But after getting to know each other better, we were still opposites but also . . . kind of . . . friends. And from the huge grin Darcy was sporting on her face, I knew Fiona had earned points with her.

Darcy and I shared a quick look and I nodded.

"Sure," Darcy said, holding a fist out.

We smiled as Fiona and I brought our fists in, and we all bumped.

Partners in Crime was expanding!

On my way to second period, I ran into Maya Doshi. I always felt like a giant tree when I stood next to her. But I really wanted to finish the conversation we'd started in the library.

"Zane told me that he's been walking you home to protect you from Hunter," I said, trying to sound casual.

"Yeah." She pulled her books close to her chest. "It's sweet of him."

"Is that the big secret you were talking about?"

Maya chewed her lip. "No."

"Can you tell me what it is?"

Maya sighed. Like she really wanted to tell me. I held my breath.

"Not yet," she whispered.

Then the bell rang and she ran off.

That night, I'd finished my homework and was checking out my favorite astronomy blog online. Mom came into the living room with a laundry basket full of clean clothes. She started to fold mine. They were all the same. Jeans, T-shirts, plain sweaters. Nothing like the cool clothes Mom wears. Nothing like Fiona's wardrobe.

"Hey, honey," Mom said. "What are you up to?"

"Um, just, you know, my thing," I said. Like she'd be interested in planetary observations.

Mom threw her head back in laughter. She has such a pretty laugh. "Can you tell me what your thing *is*?"

"Okay, sure." I cleared my throat. "Every two years, Mars comes to opposition, which means that it and the sun are on opposite sides of the sky, and Mars is closer to Earth. Which means it's easier to see in the night sky. Now is that time. It's pretty cool."

"That's interesting," she said, putting a folded sweater on top of the pile of clothes.

I went to turn back to the computer, but Mom asked, "Could you show me?"

I spun back around and smiled. "Really?"

"Yeah, let's go look through your telescope."

I jumped up and grabbed her hand. "Nope. For tonight, you only need your eyes."

I pulled her out the back door and shut off our outside light. It felt a little strange, standing in my backyard in the dark with my mother, but nice at the same time.

"Okay," I said. "Do you see the bright object up there with a bit of a red tint to it?"

She followed where I was pointing and then her face lit up when she found it. "That's it? That's a planet?"

"Yep. Mars." Then, since I had her attention, I started rattling off my favorite Mars facts. "Mars has two moons. It has higher mountains than Earth and the solar system's biggest volcano. And we think Mars used to have water but it all evaporated after the atmosphere . . ."

I stopped. Mom wasn't looking up anymore. She was staring at me.

"Wow," she said. There was a bit of awe in her voice. "It's amazing."

"Yeah, I know. And in the polar caps —"

"No, not Mars," she interrupted. "It's amazing that out of all the girls in this big, wide world . . . I ended up with the best one."

I blinked quickly, not quite knowing how to respond. Mom pulled me into a tight hug.

I wasn't the best girl in the entire universe. That was crazy talk. But my mom thought I was. And isn't that what really matters?

My heart felt as light as zero gravity. I'd solved a mystery and made a friend out of the last girl I ever thought I'd be friends with. Now, just when I thought my day couldn't get any better, I realized something else. I didn't have to have anything in common with my mom for her to be glad I was her daughter.

I hugged her even tighter.

Dad opened the door and started yelling something into the yard. I had to break up our hug to hear what he was saying.

"Did you hear me?" he yelled again. "Darcy's on the phone!"

I smirked. "You see, Mom? If I had a cell phone, Darcy could have just sent me a text and it wouldn't have interrupted our bonding moment."

"Nice try." She patted me on the head. "Go ahead and answer it. I'm going to finish up the laundry."

I ran inside and grabbed the phone off the kitchen wall. "What's up, Darcy?"

"Guess what," Darcy said quickly. She seemed excited about something.

"Chicken butt. I don't know. Tell me."

"Our detective agency just got another e-mail."

I gasped. "A threat?" I'd thought this was over!

"No, not a threat," Darcy said. I could almost hear her smiling through the line. "A new case."

Don't miss Norah and Darcy's next case!

sleuth or dare

#2: Sleepover Stakeout

Darcy, Maya, and I quietly made our way back down-stairs and sat on the couch. The TV was still on, and it cast a bluish light over the dark living room.

"I think I know what's going on," Darcy said.

Maya's eyes widened. "You do?"

"You think it's Anya," I said, and Darcy nodded.

"My sister?" Maya face scrunched up in confusion.

"She has the means and the motive," Darcy said. "She could've easily snuck into the room, whispered those words, and snuck back into her room before we got up there. All just to mess with us . . . you . . . whatever."

I usually rolled my eyes at the conspiracies Darcy came up with, but this one seemed spot-on.

"There are two problems with that theory," Maya said. "First, Anya wasn't here the other two nights I heard the voice. I was home alone with my brother."

"Maybe you thought she was out but she really snuck in to trick you?" Darcy suggested.

Maya shook her head. "I doubt that. Plus, there's the other problem. This is the third time I've heard that voice on the monitor. And it's not Anya's voice."

"How can you tell?" Darcy said. "It's fuzzy. There's

so much interference, I couldn't even tell if the voice was male or female."

Darcy was clinging to her theory, but I wasn't so sure. Maya had some good points there. Though Anya *could* have disguised her voice.

"Anya's a definite suspect," I said, "but we need to investigate other possibilities. Gather more evidence. Someone really *could* be scared, and need help. It might not be a prank."

Darcy heaved a sigh. "Yeah, you're right."

I had a thought, and turned to Maya. "Has the monitor ever picked up any other interference before?"

Maya nodded. "When we first got the monitor, it picked up the sounds of a TV show from somewhere. My parents thought it was funny."

"And it never happened again?" I asked.

"They changed the channel thingy," Maya said pointing at the back of the monitor, "and that seemed to fix it."

I picked up the monitor and saw a switch with two options: channel one and channel two. I wanted to play around with it, but didn't want to mess things up.

Darcy's face lit up. "The monitor probably couldn't pick up interference from too far away. Let's go outside and check out the neighbors, see if anyone's watching TV."

Maya wrapped her arms around her chest. "Like . . . sneak around in the dark and look in their windows?"

I understood how scary it sounded, but being a detective with Darcy had helped me become a bit braver. "We won't have to get that close," I explained to Maya. "At this time of night, people watch TV with the lights off." I pointed at the TV in front of us as an example. "All we have to do is look for the glow."

We slipped our sneakers on and headed outside. The crisp night air was chilly against my cheeks and I was really glad I'd worn a sweatshirt. We walked down the sidewalk and stopped in front of Maya's neighbor. All the lights in the house were off. "Looks like it's all dark in this one," I whispered.

"They might have a TV room in the back, though," Darcy pointed out. "We should circle the house."

Maya and I murmured in agreement. We tried to walk stealthily along the side of the house, but dead leaves and twigs kept crackling under our shoes. The moon was only a sliver of light in the black sky. Goose bumps rose up on my arms, but not from the cold.

I suddenly had the feeling we were being watched.

My eyes roamed all around . . . left, right. I was casting a nervous glance over my shoulder when I slammed into something.